Copyright

The unauthorized reproduction or distribution of a copyrighted work is illegal. Criminal copyright infringement, including infringement without monetary gain, is investigated by the FBI and is punishable by fines and federal imprisonment.

Please purchase only authorized editions and do not participate in or encourage, the piracy of copyrighted material. Your support of author's rights is appreciated.

This book is a work of fiction. Names, characters, places and incidents are the products of the author's imagination or used fictitiously. Any resemblance to actual events, locales or persons, living or dead is entirely coincidental.

Copyrighted 2022 by Delta James

Editing: Lori White Creative Editing Services

Cover Design: Dar Albert, Wicked Smart Designs

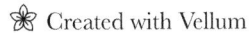

❀ Created with Vellum

JUDGMENT

SYNDICATE MASTERS: NORTHERN LIGHTS

DELTA JAMES

For Chris, Renee and the Girls:
Who make my life so much sweeter

And for Goody, who I lost during
the writing of this book. God speed
my love; you will be missed

Acknowledgements:
Editing: Lori White Creative Editing Services
Cover Design: Dar Albert, Wicked Smart
Designs

PROLOGUE

Freyja listened to the other gods bicker over petty differences. How could they ever bring peace and prosperity to those who worshipped them if they continued to squabble like greedy children? Ragnarök was coming. She needed to ensure those left behind would be protected.

Stroking the fur of the blue gray cat in her lap, she rose from her seat and removed herself from the great hall. The cat trotted off to join his brother. The two shifted from their common origins into the ice lion and the snow leopard before joining Freyja, who looked to the great boar often depicted with her. He, too, shifted and became the Winter Tiger.

"Hear me now. The gods continue to argue amongst themselves even as Ragnarök approaches. I bestow upon you three the gift of transfiguration. From beast to man, you and your descendants will be able to shape shift at will. Live among the people as human, calling upon your shifted form to lend you strength when it is needed. Watch over my people and see they do not perish from this earth."

The beasts exchanged looks with one another, their humanity already visible. As one, they emitted a soft roar, accepting their gift. Their destiny.

CHAPTER 1

Baker Street
London, England
Present Day

Lars Jakobsson left the men's locker room on the prowl. He was restless and needed to work off some steam. Sex with a beautiful submissive ought to do the trick. That's what he appreciated most about a club like Baker Street—a man like Lars didn't have to pretend he was anything other than what he was—a predatory creature that needed to lose himself with a woman who needed to submit as much as he needed to dominate.

He scented the air, his nostrils picking up the scent of aroused females. Was there any smell sweeter? The aroma filled the room, and he was glad he had decided to indulge his need. He didn't lack for sexual partners if he wanted them, but he kept them away from Runestone. It didn't do to play where he worked and lived. Runestone was a fortress, located in the hills overlooking Visby on the Swedish island of Gotland in the Baltic Sea, and had been his family's holding since 1621 when King Gustav II Adolf founded the village below that Runestone overlooked.

It had been a while since he had allowed himself the luxury of playing. If the Laochra and the Northern Lights Coalition were going to join forces, attending Braden Hughes' wedding had been a necessity. The alliance would never have been considered if his friend and ally, Gunnar Madsen, hadn't wanted to hold Joshua Knight's feet to the fire. Watching Knight squirm had almost been worth it. Watching Gunnar sling Knight's sister over his shoulder to take her back to Hammerfall had been the highlight of his day thus far. But tonight, he was sure, would prove to be far more entertaining and satisfying.

Adam Wheldon, head of security for the club, greeted him. "Lars. Were we expecting you?"

"Has Baker Street become so popular that members need to make reservations to attend?" asked Lars, arching his eyebrow.

"Not at all. I know we have Absolut on hand, but I'm not sure we've been able to get any more of the Absolut Elyx."

Lars smiled. The man was good. Hell, the whole damn club was good. He hadn't been at Baker Street in over a year and Wheldon remembered Lars' brand of vodka.

Absolut Elyx was crafted from winter wheat grown on a single estate that had been cultivating the same land for more than five centuries, then distilled in a manually operated copper column still. The spirit was known as 'liquid silk.' Served ice cold, Lars preferred it to all other liquors.

"As you said, you had no way to know I was coming."

"Let me know if you need anything."

Lars didn't answer him, but instead walked up to the lounge. He was a member of several lifestyle clubs in various parts of the world, but Baker Street was his favorite. It had a Victorian steampunk vibe to it and was well-run. He picked up a glass and a bottle of iced Absolut and headed to a dark corner in the back. It didn't do for a man like him to sit anywhere without his back to a solid wall.

A stunning blonde with violet eyes, her hair the color of honey, entered the room and a shroud of silence fell over the lounge. She glanced around, spotted him, and then took a table at the opposite end of the lounge. She was dressed in a lilac corset with raised embroidery of the same color and a matching thong. The outfit showed her curvaceous figure to its best advantage, pushing her generous tits up high and making her legs look like they went on forever. No doubt about it, the woman was smoking hot and there wasn't a man in the place who could take his eyes off her.

If the pretty prey wouldn't come to him, the predator would go to her. Picking up his bottle and his tumbler, he stopped to pick up a second glass as he approached her table.

"I appreciate a woman who can make an entrance, command all the attention in the room, and never say a word," he said, pulling a chair out and taking a seat.

"I don't remember giving you permission to join me," she said in a sultry voice that held no fear or rancor.

Her eyes held his for a moment before she lowered hers. So, she knew she was supposed to be submissive, but wasn't inclined to submit to just anyone. That was fine, Lars wasn't just anyone.

"Probably because I didn't ask."

She laughed. "Are you always this…"

"Forthright?" he interrupted.

"I was going to say rude."

"Not very submissive, are you?"

"Depends on whether or not I believe the Dom in question is man enough to dominate me."

He'd come into the club looking to find a perfectly obedient sub who would do precisely what he wanted, when he wanted, and then be on his way. Suddenly that sounded incredibly boring. He was willing to bet this woman would be anything but.

"Should I ask Adam for a private playroom, or do you prefer to play in public?"

"What makes you think I'm going to play with you?" she asked softly, leaning in just a bit so he could better see how soft and inviting her tits were.

He poured them both a shot of the vodka. Now he wished it was the Absolut Elyx he had poured her as he watched her toss it back. He lifted the bottle to question whether or not she wanted another shot. He would give her that, but then she was cut off until he was done with her. She shook her head.

He chuckled. "We both know I'm going to have you because we both know you want me, too."

"I don't even know your name."

"Lars Jakobsson, but you will call me Master."

"So, negotiation begins. I prefer to play in private and I will call you Sir."

Lars didn't like bratty subs, but she wasn't a brat. No, this was a confident woman who knew what she wanted. Luckily for him, what she wanted, if her increased arousal—evidenced by the darkening eyes, dilated pupils and stronger scent—was any indication, was to have him dominate her and ease both of their needs.

"And I will call you, *Skönhet*, which is Swedish for beauty."

"I'm flattered."

"Don't be. You're a very beautiful woman, and furthermore, you know it."

"Perhaps people tell me that and sometimes I believe them, but not always."

"Then I shall endeavor to make you believe. What are you looking for, *Skönhet?*"

"I could use some impact play."

Lars nodded. This was good. It dovetailed to his inclinations and needs. "And what do you offer in return?"

This was part of what he liked about D/s—it was a simple exchange made between consenting adults. No subterfuge, no silly romantic notions; just need for need.

"Mind-blowing sex."

She was amusing, more so than most people he met. "Sure of that, are you?" She nodded. "How do you know I can keep up?"

She eyed him up and down critically, allowing her gaze to rest on his already hard cock, which stiffened and lengthened even more. "Your reputation precedes you. I'll be honest, I was going to go watch a couple of scenes, maybe see if I could get a session from someone and go home, but several women in the submissives' salon mentioned you were here, had incredible skill with a single tail, and even more talent in the sack."

Lars tossed back his hair and laughed out loud. "You are nothing if not honest, *Skönhet*. I will be the same. I want you naked and bound to a St. Andrew's Cross; I want to leave my marks on you discreetly but so you will feel them for a few days. I will require oral and then I will fuck you silly. We will most likely be the last ones to leave the club."

He might have worried that the shiver he saw pass through her body as she sat back was fear or at least some trepidation, but his enhanced senses detected an uptick in her arousal. Lars was intrigued. It was easy for him to intimidate people, especially women. He was a mountain of a man—tall, broad-shouldered with well-defined and well-developed muscles. But he didn't detect even the slightest bit of concern on her part. She was intrigued and excited, but he doubted there was any kind of fear involved.

Lars stood, putting the top back on the vodka and extending his hand. "Come *Skönhet*."

Placing her hand in his, she rose gracefully from the chair and allowed him to lead her out. He found it curious that he thought of it as her *allowing* the action, as opposed to simply doing what she was told. Adam looked up as they left the lounge, his eyes widening in surprise.

"I didn't do anything wrong," she said preemptively to Adam.

"Do you often misbehave?" Lars asked with a chuckle.

"Misbehave?" laughed Adam. "Rhys gives JJ a run for her money in her inability to behave. She's even been known to mouth off to Fitz and earn herself some discipline, haven't you?"

She looked up at him, straightening her spine, but chewing on her lower lip. She wasn't frightened of him in the least, but she definitely wanted to enjoy his company. He doubted she had any desire to truly submit, but Lars was nothing if not capable of bending a woman, or anyone else for that matter, to his will. He wasn't known as the Guardian of Gotland for nothing.

"I believe I can handle her, can't I, *Skönhet*? If for no other reason than she wants it. Do you have one of the private rooms with a St. Andrew's Cross available?"

Adam nodded. "Both the Baskerville and Mulholland Falls are available."

"Baskerville will do fine," he said as Adam handed him the key.

He'd played in all of Baker Street's private rooms, but Baskerville was his personal favorite. It was larger with an enormous bed with a custom-built restraint system, a St. Andrew's Cross, and a large bath where a Dom could bathe and fuck a sub after an especially intense session. If things went the way he thought, he would do both.

The smile that started slowly with the slightest lifting of the corners of her mouth and spread across all of her features was bright enough to rival the Auora Borealis that danced across the sky at Runestone.

"Yes, Sir," she agreed, demurely.

Lars laughed again. His S*könhet* was anything but demure. She was most definitely what had been termed as an alpha sub. Normally, they didn't appeal to him. When he was looking to have his needs taken care of, he wanted a very submissive woman who didn't challenge and got a great deal of her needs met by servicing a Dom in any way he wanted. That was not her. No, she would get what she wanted, and he was pretty sure would top from the bottom if she wasn't paired with a true dominant alpha man. Luckily for them both, he was that kind of primal male.

Without another word, Lars turned to the curvaceous blonde, sweeping her up and over his shoulder in a singular move. She rose up, pushing herself up from his shoulder. One well-placed swat to her backside and the protest she thought to make was silenced. Good. She would learn her place from the get-go.

Lars started up the wide staircase with her firmly in place, the upper part of her body draped across his back and her ass becoming the highest part of her body. The delicious scent of her arousal filled his head. Perhaps he'd tarry in London a bit longer. He could ask to make use of one of the safe rooms or even Baskerville itself if he was willing to pay for it. Given how hard his cock was becoming, it might take more than an evening to work off his need for her.

At the top of the stairs, he turned to look down at

Adam, "Unless you have need of the room, I'll be staying at least the night."

"The room is yours until you tell me otherwise. I'll check in with your sub in the morning,"

He was feeling strong and confident and that the smack to her bottom had convinced her she would submit when she grasped his muscular buttocks and gave them a harsh squeeze. Another slap to her ass and she let go. A single tail might be on the menu, but the woman over his shoulder was in need of discipline and Lars meant to give it to her.

As alpha to his clan, he often had to provide discipline to the unmated tigresses, but he found no pleasure in doing it. It was just another job that needed to be done. But putting the woman currently riding on his shoulder over his knee and turning her pretty bottom red until she was crying and remorseful had a great deal of appeal.

Lars strode down the hall, his hand resting lightly on her ass, and thought about how it felt as though it had been made to take some serious discipline. She had a small waist and hips a man could take hold of when he fucked her. And that hair—a lovely mane of honey-colored silk that came down to the middle of her back. Plenty to fist and control her with—either holding her still as he devoured her mouth or guiding her mouth to his dick so he could feed it to her.

Reaching the end of the hall, Lars opened the door to the Baskerville room, which was decorated in luxurious Victorian debauchery, but elegant debauchery. The bed was an oversized four poster, and he could already imagine her spread eagle and tied down so he could make her squirm and struggle as he made a meal of her pussy. He hadn't realized how hungry the tiger inside him was.

CHAPTER 2

This wasn't going at all the way she'd planned. Her plan had been to accost him somewhere in London and demand that he give her answers to her questions. What the hell had happened to her sister? They were supposed to have met in Vienna to see an exhibition of the white stallions at the Spanish Riding School, but Maeve had never shown. Rhys' first calls just went to voicemail then the phone was no longer in service.

When she called the Jakobsson-owned company that was supposed to be her sister's employer, she found they would only confirm that no one named Maeve Donovan was in their employ. They would not confirm if she ever had been, and Rhys had to threaten them with a lawyer to get that much. What the company hadn't known was that Maeve was working a long-term Interpol operation, aimed at shutting down Lars Jakobsson's smuggling operations. That bit of information was classified, and Maeve could be fired or even imprisoned for having told her sister, but something about the sting had felt off to her and she wanted some kind of back-up.

When she'd flown to Stockholm a week ago to force a confrontation with those at Interpol supervising the operation, the results had been even less fruitful, and far less civilized.

"He killed my sister," snarled Rhys Donovan, slamming her fist down on the desk of the head of Interpol's office in Stockholm. She didn't know if her sister was dead, but something had happened to her, and Rhys was going to find who was responsible and make them pay. "God damn it! Do something."

"Ms. Donovan, as I've explained, I can neither confirm nor deny your sister ever having worked with or for Interpol, nor do I have any confirmation of a Maeve Donovan's death or disappearance. In fact, the only reason I know someone by that name ever lived is you have presented me with her birth certificate. I am doing you the courtesy of not questioning its validity."

Had this asshole just called her a liar?

"Listen," she snarled, looking at the nameplate on his desk, "Mr. Gustafsson— wait. Is your first name really Kermit? Kermit Gustafsson? Did your mother have a difficult labor? Or maybe she adopted you and you're the love child of Kermit the Frog and the Swedish Chef. That must be it."

"There's no reason to be insulting, Ms. Donovan," he said in a huffy tone.

Now that she looked at him, Rhys had to admit, he kind of

looked like a Kermit Gustafsson. And what was with the Swedes and all the weird double consonants? Did they and the Welsh have something in common? A language looking to buy a vowel?

"I see every reason. You people convinced my sister that you needed her help to get at Lars Jakobsson. And now she is dead, or at best missing, and you people want to play games to cover your ass and protect your operation. Well, I'm sorry, that doesn't work for me. If you won't do anything, I will."

Rhys turned around, prepared to leave his office and go find her sister. She had no idea how she was going to do that, but she was either going to find Maeve or crucify whoever had killed her. As far as she could tell, Lars Jakobsson was her primary suspect. A known mafia kingpin, he was the head of the Berserker Syndicate. Pfft, ever since the popularity of the show, everybody and their brother was claiming to be a descendant of Vikings. Well maybe he was. Rhys didn't give a damn.

Willing her tears back, Rhys threw open the door, only to be confronted by another man in an ill-fitting, bland suit, barring her exit.

"Get out of my way," *she snarled.*

"Ms. Donovan," *called Kermit,* "I'm afraid I can't let you leave in this state. Rolff, please close the door."

Rolff—she was sure his name had two Fs—reached for the handle. Feeling alone, vulnerable and worried for her sister, Rhys knew she couldn't expect any help from these people and that there was a very real possibility she'd be booted out of the country. That would add a degree of difficulty in finding her sister that she didn't need.

"Rolff," she said in warning. *"Move it or lose it. Kermit isn't going to punch you if you don't comply, but I will."*

She waited. The smug, self-satisfied smile sealed his doom. Looking him straight in the eye, Rhys punched him in the nuts, making him squeal like a pig and drop like a stone. She didn't wait to see Kermit's reaction, she just ran for the door, bolting past the elevator and down the stairs. Rhys could hear shouting behind her and the banging of the stairwell door as they gave chase. She'd seen a skybridge linking this building to the one across the street on the third floor.

Darting through the door onto the third floor, she made a mad dash for the door to the skybridge. God love the Swedes and their arrogance about having a low crime rate. Interior doors to stairwells and exits were rarely locked as long as the building itself was open. Dashing down the hall, she rushed through the door and made herself walk across the skybridge, trotting down the external stairs onto the street below, before blending in with the crowd.

She smiled hearing the shouts and vented frustration at her having eluded them. Thankfully, she had already stopped by Maeve's flat and taken all of her papers, her laptop, and several items of no real value other than to Maeve. She made her way to the closest car rental agency, rented a Volvo and merged into the traffic exiting the city in an orderly fashion.

Once she cleared the city limits, and no one was close enough behind her to see what she was doing in the car, she raised her fist and shot Stockholm her happy middle finger.

"Fuck you, Stockholm."

Rhys had flown back to London to consider her

next move. Eventually, she'd come up with a plan to somehow catch the notorious gangster alone and make him tell her what he knew about Maeve's disappearance. Rhys wasn't exactly sure how she was going to do that. Her initial plan wasn't foolproof, given their respective natures. But she was determined to get what she wanted from Lars Jakobsson, despite their normal inclinations. Maeve was the operative assigned by Interpol to their sting operation. She was trained in this sort of thing, wasn't she? Rhys, on the other hand, worked for Lloyd's of London as part of their art theft and forgery division. Her expertise in art and antiquities was second to none.

She'd known Lars was a Dom and played at Baker Street when he was in town. She hadn't lied when she told him that his reputation as both a whip and cock master preceded him. Rhys lived in London not far from the club, and played there frequently as a sub. Adam hadn't done her any favors in telling the Swedish gangster that she had been disciplined more than once for her less than submissive behavior. She also hadn't lied when she said she only submitted to those Doms she thought worthy of her submission, which she considered a great gift.

Usually, she just asked one of the Resident Doms for a session to relieve her stress. If she found them attractive, so much the better. In those instances, they could share a rollicking round of sex afterwards. If not, she made it clear from the get-go that all she would offer in return, if anything at all, was oral, and sometimes not even that. Adam had once accused her of sounding like she was ordering food from a drive thru. He wasn't far off the mark. Rhys just didn't see the big deal about sex. It was a biological imperative and hers could be as easily satisfied by her vibrator as a man… and the vibrator was less messy—physically and emotionally.

But somehow downstairs, Jakobsson had turned the tables on her. Thankfully, he thought she was fighting whether to give in and submit. That wasn't the only challenge. She battled something much greater.

Caught in the web of his sensual appeal, she was struggling to remember this man was most likely responsible for her sister's disappearance and even more likely, though she was loathe to admit it, her death. The fact was, she'd never wanted to submit completely to any man, until now. And this was the one man she couldn't afford to submit to in any way other than physical.

Right now, she would give anything she possessed to do just that. She had never found herself so wildly and completely mesmerized by a man. Lars Jakobsson was most definitely her kryptonite, but like a moth to a flame he drew her closer and closer. The question had become not whether she would submit, but whether she would survive.

CHAPTER 3

Unceremoniously he set her on her feet once he had closed and locked the door.

"On your knees, *Skönhet*."

He watched her debate in her head whether to comply with his order. The decision settled within her, and she sank to her knees with a poise, grace and, yes, arrogance he had never seen before. She was no ordinary sub, but then, he was no ordinary Dom.

"In the future, I will expect your obedience to come without the thought of rebellion. In case you missed it, I am the Dom, not you. At Baker Street the Doms may be indulgent, but they still call the shots. You either do as I command, you accept discipline when you do not, or you safe word out. What is your safe word?"

"Rembrandt."

"Interesting choice."

"I am an expert in art and antiquities for one of the major auction houses."

His interest kicked up. He knew every art expert at Sotheby's, Christie's and the like. She'd just lied to him. Not, he suspected, about her expertise but where she worked, which most likely meant she was with Scotland Yard or Interpol. What was her game? It didn't really matter. She would get no further than any of the rest, including the sassy ash blonde who'd recently tried to infiltrate his operation.

When he learned of Mara's duplicity, he had called her into the CEO's office and fired her personally, telling her he knew what she had done and sending her on her way.

Lars placed his hand on his *Skönhet's* head, holding it in place while he walked around her. Her form was perfect and her body beautiful as far as he was concerned. He was sure there were some who might find her too curvaceous, but he was not one of them. Someone had laced her corset tightly and expertly. The damn thing had to be digging into her torso, but it pushed those gorgeous tits way up high and only barely managed to contain them. It nipped in her waist and then flared out, emphasizing the natural flow of her hips. To him she was just about perfect.

He wondered if any man had ever managed to get her collared. Lars had never wanted a permanent sub, much less a mate, but as he breathed in her enticing aroma he realized where he remembered the scent. A long ago and almost forgotten memory of what his fated mate smelled like. His fated mate was human? That was, perhaps, a bit unfortunate, but not an insurmountable problem.

After completing his circle around her, he stood in front of her with his feet planted shoulder width apart. As tall as he was, she was tall enough that if she came up on her knees, she would probably be about the perfect height to suck his dick. Lars smiled. Watching his cock move in and out between those full, lush lips would be a treat, and shoving it to the back of her throat, maybe making her gag a bit as he filled her belly, would be intoxicating.

"I'm clean, *Skönhet*. Adam has my updated medicals, and I haven't touched a woman since then."

"I am, too, and I'm on birth control. If you would prefer to go bareback, I wouldn't have any objection," she said without looking up.

She had no way of knowing that until he turned her, it would be difficult, but not impossible, for her to conceive his child. Why was it, then, that the thought of her on birth control was disappointing? Was he really thinking of turning this woman he'd just met and siring offspring with her? His throbbing dick was quick to tell him the answer was a most definite yes. He wanted nothing more than to turn her, thrust his dick into her pussy, and allow his barbed cock to prepare her for his seed. The damn thing threatened to burst the laces on his leathers.

Lars realized that while she most likely needed his discipline and had asked for him to use a single-tail on her, what he really wanted was to mount her from behind and take her neck in a claiming bite. He wanted to sink his fangs down into her yielding flesh and bestow the Gift on her, take her into seclusion at Runestone and then put not just his cum, but his baby in her belly.

Taking a mate and getting her pregnant should be the last thing on his mind, and yet at the moment, it was all that he could think of... that, and the logistics involved in its accomplishment. He would need to exhaust her here at the club and then arrange to take her away from here. That might prove difficult. Baker Street was notorious about protecting its subs and no Dom, with very few exceptions, took a sub off the premises without her fully informed consent and that meant awake, sober, and coherent. He'd need to have her exhausted but lucid. Lars smiled to himself. He could do that.

Once he'd whisked her away to Runestone, there would be no one to oppose his taking her to mate. Many of his ancestors had returned from Britannia with a reluctant mate in tow. He wasn't being a manipulative bastard; he was just following tradition. Who was he kidding? He was being the Berserker of Gotland and he got to make up his own rules... rules his *Skönhet* would learn to embrace and follow.

"I want you naked, *Skönhet*," he said, once again extending his hand and helping her to stand.

Turning her away from him, he began to loosen her laces. There were times when he was impatient; he merely used his knife to cut them like a knife through butter, offering to pay to replace them as he went. He'd also cut away more than his fair share of thongs. But he was in no great hurry tonight. He intended to savor this first time—the first of many if he had his way. Lars untied the laces and began to loosen them, standing close to her so that she could feel his cut chest and substantial cock behind her. Each time he tugged the laces, she was forced a bit closer. God, she smelled sweet.

Finally, the corset was loose enough that he could pull it over her head, revealing that it had been laced far too tight, the boning leaving red grooves in her skin. He wasn't opposed to marks as long as he made them with some kind of whip or with his bindings and they didn't mar the perfection of a woman's skin permanently. He didn't object to any scars a sub came by in the course of her life. They showed she had endured and survived. Lars turned her back around to face him, brushing her long hair over her shoulders so that nothing hid the beauty of her breasts. They were exceptional, with dark, dusky areolas and stiffened nipples that begged to be sucked, but that would come later.

"I have named you well, *Skönhet*. You are quite beautiful."

She looked up to lock eyes with his and acknowledged her master, and then lowered them. So, she could feel it too. Being human, she wouldn't understand it for what it was, but he knew. His mate had instinctively recognized she was in the presence of her fated mate and had begun to yield. Depending on how well she served him, she might escape his discipline this time.

Lars wasn't known for his patience, but he would show her that he could be. Part of him wanted to rip the thong off her, tossing her onto the bed and covering her with his body. He'd part her legs, settling himself before shoving his cock up inside her, claiming her in the same way men and shifters had been claiming their mates for ages. But any man with a functioning cock could do that. It took a real man, a Dom, to gain her trust, her consent, and her desire to give herself over to him completely. Lars meant to have all of that from her.

Her words that she only submitted to a man who was Dom enough to take her had been a taunt and nothing more. Oh, it had been true enough, but it had been the challenge of an alpha sub whose need to be conquered was as great as his need to conquer her.

Lars nodded at the only remaining item of her clothing. "Take them off."

She said nothing but placed her hand on his chest

to balance herself and removed them. He wondered idly if she'd studied dance. She moved with the strength and grace of a ballerina. She must have studied for years and been disappointed when she'd grown so tall and developed that rack. Screw being a ballerina, he had much better plans for her, especially where those tits were concerned.

"Knees. Hands behind your back."

This time she obeyed without question. *Good girl.* He unlaced his leathers, opening the front and freeing his rampant cock. The thing actually ached, he wanted her so bad. Lars knew he had a quick recovery time and so would take his pleasure before giving her the lash and then fucking her silly until she was exhausted and compliant. An excellent plan, if he did say so himself.

His cock dripped pre-cum, and she moistened her lips with her tongue.

"Lick it up," he rumbled, enjoying the way the sound seemed to tumble along her skin, the natural link between them already coming to life.

He placed the bulbous head right in front of her and obligingly her tongue darted out, catching the slightly salty essence before it could leave his dick. He barely managed to hold back a groan. God, she felt good.

"Now take me and take me deep."

His mate sucked his cock into her mouth, drawing him in. The sight of her lips wrapped around him as she swirled her tongue all over his tightened skin was almost enough to undo him.

"Deeper," he said, pressing into her.

She tried to pull back, tried to evade his reaching the soft, velvety place at the back of her throat. The fingers of one hand reflexively sank into her hair, tightening and holding her in place as he fed her his staff. He knew he was larger than most and could be a bit hard to take all the way, but she would do it. She would swallow him down and revel in the feel of his cum sluicing down her throat.

His beauty relaxed her jaw and steadied her breathing, allowing him to invade her mouth and take his fill of her. She traced the sensitive frenulum on the underside of his cock, using the tip of her tongue to tease him before sucking him deep, letting him press all the way to the back.

"Yes," he groaned, as his other hand came up, tangled in her hair and held her immobile and helpless in his grasp.

Lars focused on the feel of her mouth surrounding him as he began to fuck it, pumping his hips and letting his balls bump against her chin. She was focused on the underside of his cock, probably because she couldn't get her tongue on him anywhere else. As he thrust deep, she swallowed him down, triggering his release as he muffled a roar and spurted his cum down her throat.

She didn't flinch, didn't lose a drop. She sucked

him down and swallowed everything he had to give her. When he softened the grip on her head, she didn't pull away, just licked and cleaned him with long passes of her tongue as he gently stroked in and out.

This time he said, "Good girl. Now let's see what I can do for you with a single-tail."

He placed his cock back inside his leathers, lacing them closed and helping her to stand. He led her to the St. Andrew's cross, binding her to it. Lars noticed her body was languid and soft and the scent of her arousal had increased yet again. He bound her tightly enough that she wouldn't be able to move in a way that might get her hurt. She might not want to admit it, but his mate had a submissive streak a mile wide. She just needed the right man to help her embrace that. Luckily for her, she'd found him. She was so relaxed, which was good, but a little anticipation of what was to come would help her find subspace. It would also kick start his own libido so when she was ready, he would fuck her into ecstasy and beyond. He would take her places no other man ever could.

Biting her lower lip, she tested the restraints and he let her be. Not touching or speaking to her, he backed away, keeping an eye on her as he reached for the single-tail in his kit. He inhaled deeply, savoring the scent of her arousal, now tinged with worried anticipation. There was no fear, just the understanding that before the pleasure, the initial stroke of the whip would sting, giving them both a rush of desire zinging through their veins.

Taking hold of the handle, he unfurled the whip, swishing it back and forth and giving it a single snap away from her body, grinning as she flinched. Anticipation was sweet, but satisfaction was so much better. With every flick of the lash, it was as if all the planets were coming into alignment. The alignment of things that had always been fated.

CHAPTER 4

He drew back and allowed the tail of the whip to find its target, giving her a quick lick of the lash, making her skin contract and the muscles in her ass tense.

"You know better, *Skönhet*. It will only increase the sting of the whip if you tighten up. Trust me, *Skönhet*. I will see you get what you need." *And then some.*

He raised the whip, bringing it back down across the major muscles in a dance of pleasure and pain. She moaned with each strike and gradually her entire body relaxed as she sagged into the framing, her breathing becoming steady, deep, and even as he continued to move the whip around, covering her body, leaving little raised weals here and there.

"Are you with me, *Skönhet*?" he asked, stilling the single-tail.

She nodded.

"Words, *Skönhet*. I need words."

"Yes, Sir," she managed to sigh with a dreamy tone.

He chuckled low. "I will teach you to call me Master," he purred, loving the way her body trembled from the verbal caress.

Placing his hand on what would be her withers once she was a tigress, he steadied her, releasing her from her bonds, turning her around and binding her back into place.

"Sir?" she questioned, not with concern, but a lazy curiosity.

"I haven't had my fill of you yet."

She glanced down at the bulge pressing against the front of his leathers. "You seem recovered, Sir."

Even hovering in subspace, she still had the capacity to sass him. He'd teach her to mind her mouth, or he'd place a ball gag on her and do it for her.

"Bad *Skönhet*," he said, smiling at her.

Lars ran his hand down her body, briefly cupping each of her breasts and bending down to give one a quick suckle. No doubt about it, he was going to spend some serious time worshiping those beauties. She was groomed properly and was bare and slick. He rubbed his knuckles across her clit, and she shivered again.

"Someday, I will teach you to come just from the lash."

He flattened his palm and rubbed it over her mons, noting that she was getting wetter and if her nipples were any indication, more aroused by the moment. Fisting her hair, he tilted her head back, realizing as he lowered his head, he meant to kiss her. Kissing was not something he normally did with a sub in a club. Too many of them interpreted it to mean more than he wanted. But she was his mate, she should start learning that tonight was just the first of all the nights to come.

His fingers parted her labia and slipped easily up into her cunt. She bit her lower lip again, obviously fighting her need to come.

"It's all right *Skönhet*. I don't want you to hold back. I enjoy hearing you come."

"You've never heard me come, Sir," she said with a bit of disrespect.

Lars took no offense and recognized it for what it was, simply her way of trying to keep her equilibrium. He wasn't about to allow that.

"You will give over and come for me as often as I like," he purred in her ear, standing close and beginning to thrust his fingers in and out.

She caught her breath, trying to regulate her response. But she was not in charge; he was, and she would yield to him. Continuing to stroke her pussy, he used the ball of his palm to press down on her clit and she lost control, crying out his name as the rush of her orgasm coated his hand.

"Such a good girl," he said, standing in front of her and leaning down to release the ankle restraints. He stood close to her, pressing her lightly into the frame of the cross before releasing her wrists. She sagged against him, her arms wrapping around him to steady herself. "I've got you *Skönhet*. I'll always catch you."

Swinging her up into his heavily muscled arms, he crossed to the bed, sitting down on the edge and holding her in his lap. Purring to her and rubbing her back, he let her relax and recover. When she made to move from his lap, he pinched her clit, and she sank back into him.

"Not until I say," he growled.

"Yes, Sir."

"I want you in the middle of the bed, facing the headboard, on your knees and forearms, ass high." She didn't know it, but after he'd fucked her thoroughly, he meant to stretch out next to her while she slept. He wouldn't sleep; he would keep watch over her. He never slept with subs, but, he reminded himself, she was his mate.

She crawled out of his lap and positioned herself as he'd commanded. He moved up behind her, rubbing his hands lightly across her ass, which would definitely bear his mark for a few days, before gripping her hips.

He reached between her legs to ensure she was still ripe and ready, smiling as he confirmed that if anything, she was even wetter, and her little love nub was even more swollen. He ran his hand down her spine, splitting her long mane and allowing it to drape over her shoulders, leaving the nape of her neck bare. He wasn't really thinking of claiming her here at Baker Street, was he?

Before the question could even form properly, he could feel his fangs beginning to elongate. He had a passing thought that he ought to wait, ought to get her accustomed to the idea, but decided there was no need. She was his and he might as well make her so. Generally, a claiming bite put the recipient into a highly aroused and dreamy state, the endorphins and changes to their DNA reacting almost immediately. She was already there. No reason not to enjoy her to the fullest.

He pulled her ass towards him, angling his cock so that he could impale her with it. He might inflict the claiming bite here, but he would not allow the barbs out until they were back home in Runestone. The head of his cock was poised for a fraction of a moment before he pushed in and began to breach her.

Slowly he entered her, only to draw back and then press forward again, making her gasp in exaggerated pleasure. Ah, so his mate liked the feel of his cock as he took her for the first time. Good. She would need to get used to being mounted several times a day. He withdrew almost completely before driving into her, not brutally, but with enough force that her pussy had no choice but to accommodate him as she climaxed again just from his complete possession.

The human part of his brain reminded him that he needed to explain who and what he was and obtain her consent before initiating the Gift. It had always been that way. A tiger obtained the consent of a human before turning them. Lars had never been much for following others' rules and conventions, though, and saw no need to start now. The Winter Tiger within reminded him that she was his fated mate and would be his, damn the consequences or her consent.

As he began thrusting in and out, holding her so that she didn't collapse from the onslaught of his passion, the predatory beast beat back the civilized man and allowed his fangs to elongate. He would take…he would claim her in the primal way of their kind… she was one of them.

He surged in and out with a raw, ruthless rhythm that gave her no respite. She clutched at the bedsheets and pillows, trying to exert some kind of control. Lars had no intention of relinquishing it. He pounded into her with a ruthless abandon; it was a new experience for him. He prided himself on the fact that he never succumbed to the rapture to be found in fucking a woman. He was always in control, but claiming his mate was another thing entirely. He fucked her hard and possessively, reveling in the way she cried out his name over and over again as he lost himself to the ecstasy he found in forcing her to climax repeatedly.

Holding her in place, he refused to allow her to move with him. She needed to learn who did the fucking and who got fucked. Repeatedly, he thrust in and out, finding her sweet spot and drawing his cock across it until she was spent, collapsing in his hands as the pleasure surged through her, ensuring her complete and utter exhaustion.

As he felt the tension in her body beginning again, he knew it was now or never, leaning over her back, wrapping his arm around her at the juncture of her legs with her torso to hold her close, he leaned on his other arm to keep some of his weight from her and bent down to her neck. He nuzzled it lovingly, softly kissing each spot where he knew his fangs would sink deep. Harder and deeper he thrust until she cried out in final surrender, and he bit down savagely, making her scream into the pillow.

This was no time for gentleness or sweet words. This was the claiming bite of the Winter Tiger and she would submit and be forever changed by it. He loosened his jaw for a moment before sinking his fangs even deeper. This time she did not scream, she merely went limp, too exhausted to do anything else as he began to pump his seed deep inside her.

Her pussy contracted up and down his length, encouraging him to fill her with his cum. He continued to thrust, until he spurted all of himself into her and her cunt had milked him dry. He allowed her to collapse and fell on top of her, allowing the mattress to cushion her body as she provided a soft place for him to rest.

Lars rolled to his back, drawing her close to his side, wrapping his arm around her and wedging his leg between her thighs. She struggled weakly and briefly before her body succumbed to the gentle resonance of his purring and her exhaustion. Never before had he experienced such ecstasy. He had not thought it possible.

He chuckled softly. He would have to remember to apologize for all the things he'd said to his second-in-command over the years. Lars had never believed he would have a fated mate and had thought it romantic drivel. He'd been wrong and he meant to bask in this feeling for the rest of his life.

~

Holy Mary, Mother of God, what have I done? Why did I ever think playing with a man like Jakobsson would work?

The plan was to lull him into a feeling of security and then figure out what he knew about her sister's disappearance. Instead, she had let him take control. Granted it had been the most amazing session she'd ever experienced. She knew all about subspace, at least in theory, but she had never been able to achieve it. What she did experience was a kind of deep relaxation combined with an exponential amount of lust that she usually relieved for herself after she got home. That way when the orgasm was still buzzing through her system, it would provide for a deep and restorative sleep.

After the first time, she hadn't so much fallen asleep as collapsed from a combination of sheer exhaustion and being completely and totally blissed out. She might have been able to recover at least her dignity if he hadn't reached for her repeatedly, pulling her beneath him and starting the cycle all over again. The man's reputation did not adequately express his talent with the single-tail, much less with his cock. She'd had sessions with so-called 'whip masters' before, and they had been nice, but not the overall encompassing experience she'd had with Lars.

Sometime shortly before dawn, she managed to slip out of his embrace, leaving the corset behind and wrapping a blanket around her before quietly opening and closing the door. Making her way to the submissives' salon, Rhys changed quickly and made use of the discreet exit JJ had shown to the submissives who played at Baker Street regularly. The Doms hated that they couldn't find it, which made it all the more fun to use.

The cold, gray light and damp fog suited her mood. She felt as if she had failed her sister and herself completely. *He's a gangster,* she reminded herself. The reputed syndicate master of Gotland and one of the main cogs in the wheel of art thefts and forgeries. Jakobsson wasn't responsible for either, but he did facilitate getting them from one place to another, and no one had a clue as to how. Maeve's job had been to find out, set him up, and bust his cartel wide open.

It hadn't happened, and now Maeve was missing.

CHAPTER 5

The gentle rapping on the door wormed its way into his subconsciousness. A little louder knock and he came fully awake, sitting up and feeling the cold, empty bed beside him. He glanced at the bath. The door was open, and he could neither hear, nor see her. He scented the air and could detect only a lingering aroma from when she had been with him. Damn!

The third time the person outside knocked, it was accompanied by the sound of a key being inserted into the lock. Double damn! Now Wheldon would know she had slipped out on him; no one else would dare disturb him.

Worse than Wheldon knowing she'd bested him—at least for now—was concern for her safety. She had no way of knowing what had happened to her. If she had stayed in bed with him, he could have taken her to Runestone and begun to teach her what it was to be a tigress. More than that, the mate to the Winter Tiger.

What made her think she was free to leave his bed? How the hell had she managed that? He would ensure she couldn't do so in the future. He had to find her. How the hell was he going to convince the club to give him her name? He realized now how deftly she had avoided revealing her name. Lars knew he had been played, although to what extent was still unknown.

If Wheldon gave him any shit about not looking after her properly, Baker Street would be looking for a new manager and Resident Dom. If he took any grief over this, he would drag her back by the roots of her hair and make her apologize for her foolishness.

"Lars?"

"Come in, Adam. I'm here by myself," he said, rolling out of bed and pulling on a pair of the sweatpants Baker Street provided in all sizes in all the rooms.

"Oh, I didn't expect that," Adam said as he entered the room and looked around to confirm she wasn't there. "I mean what you and your sub do is up to the two of you, but when you said you wanted the room for the night, I just expected…"

"You expected what I expected—exactly what we both should have expected. It would seem my sweet sub has decided to play a game of hide and seek. She will find I do not lose what is mine."

"Take it easy, Jakobsson. If she didn't want to stay, that was her call. I'm a bit surprised she did so without telling you, but then that, too, was her call." Wheldon rubbed his chin. "I probably owe her an apology."

"No, she will apologize to you. I can see you are concerned for her safety. If she wanted to play games with me, that's one thing. Causing you concern is quite another. Don't let it trouble you further. I assure you I will find her and make sure she's all right."

"That's all well and good, but I didn't have a chance to confirm with her what she wanted. She seemed comfortable with you, but I feel as though I neglected her by not confirming that. I was actually going to ask if you want breakfast delivered."

"No, but thank you. I need to get after her. I don't suppose you'd be inclined to give me her address, would you?" No need for Wheldon to know he didn't even know her name.

"Sorry, Lars, you know the rules…"

"I do, but if you see her, ask her… no scratch that. Tell her I told you to tell her to get in touch with me. The club has my private mobile number. I would appreciate you seeing she gets it."

"Look, I don't know what went on or what was said between you, but generally when a woman slips out, she isn't looking for a rematch."

Lars growled low in his throat and Adam stepped back.

"Apologies," said Lars, waving Adam off. "You're not deserving of my ire, but I promise you the next time you see my *Skönhet*, she'll be at my side with my ring on her finger and my collar around her neck. This is just some bullshit game she's playing and when I catch up with her, she won't sit for a week."

Adam tried to hide a grin and failed. "I know it won't help much, but I know the feeling, and so does Fitz. JJ led him on a merry chase before he got a ring on her finger and a collar around her neck. More than one Dom has had to jerk a knot in the tail of his sub before she decided to settle down. Just see that anything non-consensual stays away from the club."

Lars nodded. "Understood."

What Wheldon had no way of knowing was that his S*könhet* was his fated mate. More than that, her DNA was undergoing a profound change. Lars needed to find her and take her home. And he needed to do it sooner rather than later. There were those who would seek to harm him through her. She had no way of knowing that, either. He was a man with enemies, and she could be a helpless pawn if the wrong people learned of her importance to him.

Normally, the transition from human to tiger-shifter just involved a mild malaise for a day or two, nothing more distressing than a slight case of the flu, but that wasn't always the case. Rhys or any doctor she saw would have no idea what was happening to her. What concerned Lars more than either of those scenarios was that once the transition was complete, if she was threatened, her tigress might come to the fore in order to protect her. And then, depending on where it happened, all kinds of hell could break loose.

Grabbing his leathers and boots, Lars started to leave, but turned back and scooped up her corset to take with him. He jogged down the stairs, entered the men's locker room and called for a town car. After changing into his street clothes, he left Baker Street and once inside the car, asked the driver to take him to the Tin Whistle, a restaurant that specialized in breakfast and brunch, which was open from five in the morning until two in the afternoon. Glancing at his watch he realized the place would be packed, so he asked the driver to let him out at the rear entrance.

Knocking on the door, a very annoyed hostess opened it—her expression changing immediately upon seeing who it was.

"Mr. Jakobsson, how lovely to see you. Please come in. I'll try and get you a table as quickly as possible. Did I miss your reservation?"

"No, Penny, you didn't. And truthfully, if I could just borrow the employee privacy room for about half an hour, I need to place a sensitive call. Then I'll sit anywhere you want me to, and you can feed me leftovers."

Penny blushed prettily, brought the back of her

thumb up to rest on her plump lower lip and lowered her eyes. She was a lovely girl and more than once he'd thought about playing with her at Baker Street. But she was new to the lifestyle, and he rather imagined she was more interested in pursuing her crush on him than she was in embracing her submissive side, which truth to tell was more than evident to even a casual observer.

"I think we can do better than that. You know your way, don't you? We're slammed this morning so I'll put in an order for you unless you want something other than your usual, and someone will bring it back to you. Can I get you tea or coffee or something else to drink?"

"Coffee with my breakfast is fine, and I do apologize for my intrusion and the extra work."

"It's no trouble, Mr. Jakobsson. Chef has made it clear that you are always welcome and are to be extended every courtesy."

Lars smiled as he headed back to the employees' lounge. He was quite sure the chef had been very specific about that; for one thing, the chef was a member of Lars' clan and for the second, Lars was the majority owner of the restaurant. It had been one of his shrewder, legal investments. The place was packed every morning and made money hand-over-fist.

He let himself into the empty lounge and closed himself in the small privacy room. The room had been created so employees could place private phone calls without having to go outside or find a broom closet.

He dialed Björn back at Runestone. It was seven in the morning in London, which meant it was eight in the morning at home. He was sure Björn would be up, especially in Lars' absence.

"We expected you last night. But when I remembered you said you were going to Baker Street, I thought maybe you found a girl to spend some time with. When I called there this morning to confirm your whereabouts, I got the usual runaround. Adam Wheldon finally admitted you were there. I practically had to give blood and promise him my first-born."

Lars smiled. "I wouldn't expect anything less of Baker Street. The club is very discreet and takes confidentiality seriously. How is Britt feeling?"

"No kidding about their stand on protecting their members. I threatened a physical confrontation with our men, which frankly didn't seem to impress him overly much. It then occurred to me to call Joshua Knight. As he is a member, Wheldon would confirm that you had been there. And Britt is over hating me and feeling miserable in the mornings. We are now in the behaving like an alley cat in heat, which I must say is a great deal more pleasurable for me. Honestly though Lars, it's awful when they're feeling sick, and you can do nothing for them. And although I know you love my Britt, I very much doubt that's why you called."

"You would be correct. Did you find out anything more about the woman we caught sticking her nose in places it shouldn't have been? And I need boots on the ground here, but discreetly."

"About the woman? Yes, and it's not good. As to the other, wouldn't it be easier to simply ask for Knight's help?"

"I have no wish to involve Joshua Knight in my private affairs. But I need to slip a number of men into the country who can blend in and conduct a search. And what do we know about Mara Donahue?"

"Well, we know that isn't her real name. Her name is actually Maeve Donovan, and she does work for Interpol. She's part of their art theft and forgeries division."

"Shit! I knew they were making another run at us."

"They don't like you very much," said Björn. Although he couldn't see him, Lars could well imagine the grin on Björn's face.

"The feeling is mutual. Let's lie low for a bit and keep our operations small for a while. Let's give Interpol some time to decide we're either too dull or too difficult to crack until they decide to go after someone else. Do we know where Maeve or Mara is?

Those idiots at the dock managed to let her get away."

"I know. As bad as her working for Interpol is, that isn't the worst of it."

"What could be worse? Neither of the other parties to the transaction knew; we were the only ones," said Lars, clenching his fist as his voice rose in anger and concern.

"Apparently not. We found a listening device at the exchange site. Very well hidden."

"Interpol?"

"Doubtful. I think it's more likely that it was either the buyer or the seller."

"Fuck. We need to find her. I'll reach out to our contacts at Interpol. You start trying to track her and keep in touch."

"Will do. The other plane is leaving with our men. Where do you want them to meet you?"

"I'll meet them at the private airstrip north of London that we always use. The owner owes me a favor and is an incurable romantic; I'm sure he'll let us use the abandoned hangar like he did before. I'll send the smaller plane back to you."

"Are you sure I shouldn't join you? What's going on?"

Lars sighed. "No, you need to stay with Britt and take care of her and the rest of our clan at Runestone. I'll join you as soon as I can, and I'll see what I can't find out from our friends at Interpol."

"Lars, what's going on with you?"

Another sigh. This was not a conversation he was going to enjoy having with Björn. He knew his friend and beta would understand, but when she was back in his arms and home at Runestone, Björn was going to have a field day giving him shit.

"Let me start by saying, you were right. Fated mates do exist."

Björn started to chuckle. "Good God, don't tell me it's one of Knight's lionesses…"

"It would be so much easier if it were."

"I wouldn't think so. What could be worse than that?"

"She's human and she doesn't know about our kind."

"Okay, not ideal, but not an insurmountable problem. Tigers have been turning human females for thousands of years. Are you planning to bring her here first? Did you have a fight? What did you do?"

"You know, you're beginning to sound a lot like your mate," Lars grumbled. Then seeing no reason not to tell him, he said, "I claimed her."

"What do you mean 'claimed her?'"

"I mean precisely what you think I mean. I was having sex with her, took her by the nape of her neck, and sank my teeth into her."

"And you lost her? How the fuck did you do that?"

"I lost my head to your romantic notions and seized the moment and her neck."

"Then how did she get away?"

"Apparently my tiger was so relieved to know we had her that we slept soundly enough that she slipped out of our bed. So now I need to find her and bring her home."

"Oh shit, Lars. I don't know whether to laugh at you, commiserate with you, or tell you that is the single stupidest thing you've ever done, which is saying a lot because I know most, if not all, of the stupid things you've done. Christ, what if…"

"Enough," growled Lars. "I have done nothing but berate and what if'd myself until I'm physically ill."

"Apologies, Alpha," Björn said, respectfully. "I can only imagine how upset you are. We'll find her. Do you have a picture?"

"No, but I have an idea of how to get one. Tap into the CCTV around Baker Street, sometime between four and six this morning. You're looking for a tall, long-legged, long-haired honey-colored blonde with an hourglass figure. You probably won't be able to tell, but she has the most amazing violet eyes. I have no idea what she'll have on. Do a screen capture of any woman matching my general description and send it to me. I'll recognize her. Once we have that we can run her through the government's records to see if we can find her. Start with the passport office."

"Will do. Once you confirm it's her, I'll send her

picture to the men. Do you want them to come to you?"

"No. I think it's imperative that we have a place to set up shop privately. I don't want Knight knowing or becoming involved. We have to find her."

"We will, Alpha. You will be reunited with your mate and have her in your arms as quickly as it's possible to do so."

Lars ended the call, just as his breakfast and a strong cup of coffee were brought to him. He barely tasted either before he left money on the table for the food and a generous tip and then ducked out the employee entrance, hailing the town car he'd hired earlier.

Waiting for it to pull up, he rolled his shoulders and his neck, trying to unkink the knots that had taken up residence there.

When I find you Skönhet, you will rue the day you tried to run from me.

He got into the SUV and headed out of town. It was going to be a long day, and something told him, longer still until he had her back in his arms where she belonged.

CHAPTER 6

Lars directed the town car to the airport, raised and locked the partition between the front and back and placed his call to their man in Interpol. It was an uneasy alliance to say the least. For his part, Lars never asked him to do anything illegal save confirming something Lars already knew. He also ensured it could never be traced back to their mole. In exchange, the man's daughter, who had been dying of leukemia, had been made a tigress and was an integral part of Lars' clan. The transition process was known to cure most human ailments, including diseases of the blood and cancers. The Interpol agent might know of their existence, but he couldn't give them away without condemning his own child. And that, Lars was sure, he would never do.

The drive to the airport was smooth and gave Lars time to do what he needed, including engaging a helicopter service that had a helipad in Central London. He arranged to have a chopper sitting on standby for his use should he need it and to have four SUVs delivered to the airport. Once his men arrived, they'd divide the city into quarters and begin a systematic search for her until they could run down information that would tell them who she was and where to focus their search.

Once at the airport, Lars was able to offer the owner enough cash to allow him to rent the deserted hanger for as long as he needed it… no questions asked. The SUVs arrived shortly before his men did. Once they touched down, Lars sent their other pilot with the smaller plane back to Runestone.

Lars divided up the city into quadrants and then his men into four groups, with each assigned to a specific section of the city. Lars took the area closest to Baker Street. The one thing they had already been able to confirm was that there had been no for-hire transportation used in the area during the timeframe needed.

Just as they were pulling off to head back into the city, his mobile phone buzzed. It was Björn.

"Our man at Interpol confirmed Mara was one of theirs. And confirmed her real name—Maeve Donovan. So, while I'm here, I need you to step up the search to find her. I think her bosses sent the little guppy in to swim with the sharks. I fear she got gobbled up," said Lars as he answered the phone.

"I fear you are right," said Björn. "I don't understand why humans seem to think nothing of sacrificing their women this way." He sighed. "But, on a better note, I think we've got your mate. I just sent you her picture to confirm, but I already had our men run her face through the systems. The good news is, we got a hit."

"The bad news?" Because Lars knew there was always bad news.

"If the woman whose picture I sent you is your mate, then our searches have become interrelated."

Lars glanced down at his mobile. Björn had been right to start the search. It was indeed his beautiful fated mate. "That's her. Well done."

"Don't congratulate me yet. I was really hoping I was wrong. Your fated mate's name is Rhys Donovan and she has an older sister named Maeve."

It was all Lars could do not to physically recoil. He felt as though he'd been punched in the gut. "Shit. Send me all you have on Maeve, and we'll track her down from this end. Start combing the hospitals and morgues between here and there, including Paris, Berlin, Copenhagen, and Stockholm."

"You think she's dead?" asked Björn.

"Dead or hurt. My guess is Rhys—that's her name, right? Rhys?"

"Yes, Alpha."

"I suspect she knew precisely who I was before she ever walked into Baker Street. If Maeve is still alive, and I do not want to greet my mate with news of her sister's death, Interpol will know where she lives. Get someone there and make sure Maeve didn't get home without our knowing. Then have him wait for her."

"If Maeve is there or he sees her?"

"Get her to Runestone. If she's in the hospital, get her out and get her transported home. If necessary, we will turn her to save her life."

"Yes, Alpha."

Lars ended the call, banged the back of his head on the headrest, closing his eyes and pinching the bridge of his nose. What had started earlier in the day as a casual game of cat and mouse had just turned into a clusterfuck of the first order.

∽

Rhys had tried to go about her day as best she could. She'd run by her house, taken a quick shower and put on fresh clothes. It still seemed to her that she could smell him on her skin. What had she been thinking? She was no Interpol operative—she was no kind of operative at all. The fact was, she did most of her work examining artwork suspected of being forgeries or verifying their authenticity either for a private sale, an auction or to be exhibited in a museum or gallery from a desk space in the basement of the Lloyd's building. She didn't even have a cubicle.

She and her sister had been born in London. She rarely left the United Kingdom—twice for business trips—one in Dublin, one in New York City, and a surprise visit to her sister's flat in Lyon. The trip to Vienna, the one where she waited for days for her sister to contact her, had been her most exotic trip. But Maeve had never shown.

Rhys might not be a trained investigator, but she knew a lie or prevarication when she heard one. When she'd called to check on her sister, the Interpol office in Stockholm had wanted to play 'wink-wink-Bob's-your-uncle.' That had been her first mistake, going to the office. No doubt after her altercation with Interpol, there was some kind of alert or warrant out for her. As she'd sat in her office day-after-day, she'd winced every time the door opened, expecting the authorities to drag her off in handcuffs, her bosses firing her as Interpol led her away.

But what the hell was she supposed to do? Interpol was doing nothing, so if someone was going to find and save Maeve, it was going to have to be her. The problem was, she didn't know the first thing about tracking her sister's whereabouts. Rhys knew from her own experience that Lars Jakobsson controlled most of the smuggling of stolen and forged art out of his fortress on Sweden's Gotland Island. Runestone.

When she read that Jakobsson would be in Wales for Braden Hughes' wedding, she'd thought it might be an ideal time to 'just happen' to run into him. She'd been a member of Baker Street for years. She preferred her sex to be transactional as opposed to having to bother with relationships. She'd convinced one of the receptionists at Baker Street to let her know when Lars was expected. She'd promised her that she had no nefarious plans for the gorgeous Swede, but of course she was lying. Rhys was convinced that Maeve's life was at stake. She was prepared to do a lot more than lie.

Rhys had barely made it into the office on time, trying to slip in unobtrusively and going right to work. She'd been examining the craquelure on a Raphael painting that Lloyd's had been sent to verify its authenticity. Rhys was beginning to suspect it was a forgery—a clever and well done one, but a forgery, nonetheless. Craquelure was the network of fine cracks that developed over time on the surface of a painting, caused chiefly by the shrinkage of the paint or varnish.

While the painting did show craquelure, it was man made in regular, predictable patterns over the surface of the painting. Craquelure that develops over the years exhibits random and irregular patterns. The network of cracks was neither random nor irregular. Rhys was convinced it was a fake. But she would need more than craquelure to definitively make that statement.

Time to move on to examining the actual paints used as well as its visual style. The notion that painters had one style, that might develop differently over time, had long been held as a reliable method of verifying art. The visual style of the painting was reminiscent of Raphael, but Rhys wasn't convinced it wasn't just a clever forger imitating the brush strokes of a master.

Then there was the painting's questionable provenance. The painting had supposedly disappeared along with hundreds of thousands of other paintings and pieces of art during World War II. The Nazis had been notorious for 'confiscating,' 'acquiring,' and 'liberating' priceless pieces of art, many of which were still missing, which allowed disreputable art dealers, artists, and thieves to claim what they had was worth millions.

Deep in thought, she rubbed the back of her neck and found two small abrasions. They felt like puncture wounds. When the hell had that happened? And what had caused them? She'd take a look at them tonight when she got home. She vaguely remembered feeling a pinch on her neck when Jakobsson had been fucking her. Had the sonofabitch bitten her?

Contemplating how they would break the news to the owner that he or she had paid a fortune for a fake,

Rhys all but jumped out of her skin when Laura Pritchard came up beside her, putting her hand on Rhys' shoulder. Rhys knew from talking to Laura, who was both a friend and colleague and who had been responsible for the painting coming to Lloyd's for authentication, that it wouldn't be so much the money lost, but rather the connection to the family who had perished during the war that would be the bitter pill.

"What?" Rhys said, breathing heavily. "God, Laura, you about scared me to death."

"Are you all right?"

Rhys glanced down at her clothing. Everything appeared to be in the right order. "Why? Don't I look all right?"

"You look great. You always do, but you weren't here when I got in this morning…"

"I was on time."

"Just barely, and you're always here before I am. Your skin looks clammy." Laura pressed her palm to Rhys' forehead and then to each cheek. "I'm worried about you."

"Thanks. I'm just feeling a little off. I might be coming down with something, or maybe it's too many years sniffing paint fumes."

Laura laughed. "How's it going with our friend Raphael?"

Rhys shook her head. "Not good. I don't think it's

real. The visual style is a bit off. If everything else was right, I might be inclined not to give that a lot of weight, but the craquelure is way off and the provenance is a bit iffy. I'm going to take a couple of paint samples, but the forgers are getting better and better about getting that part right."

"Do you ever wonder why some of these forgers who are really, really talented don't just apply that talent to original work of their own?" asked Laura, frowning.

"Perhaps they don't have the imagination to come up with an original idea."

"You could be right," Laura said as if trying to puzzle something out. "Seriously, if you're not feeling well, go home. If you're worried about a deadline, why not email your notes home, write it up there on your laptop, and email it back. That way you can get it done and get some rest while you're doing it."

Rhys stood; when a wave of dizziness swept over her, she steadied herself with her hand on the desk. "You know, I think I'm going to take your advice. I'll let them know I'm going."

"Take care. Let me know if you want me to pick up take-away for you and drop it at your flat. Anton is taking me to dinner so it would be easy enough to stop by your place."

"Thanks, Laura. I may take you up on that."

They both knew she wouldn't. Rhys didn't care for Laura's boyfriend, Anton Petrov, who owned a small but prestigious gallery. Not as prestigious as he'd like people to believe, which was part of Rhys' dislike of the man. Ever since he and Laura had become an item, Rhys had seen less and less of her friend.

Rhys tidied up her workspace, putting the painting back in the vault, and decided against emailing her notes. She pretty much knew what she wanted to say in her progress report and could finish it up tomorrow. Locking the vault behind her, Rhys picked up her things and took the lift from the basement where the art was housed, and the work completed. Pushing open the glass door, she breathed in the fresh air and headed for home.

She was only knocking off an hour early and hadn't taken a lunch break, so technically she had put in a full day. If she hurried, she could stop by one of the high-end corsetiers to get an idea for what a new corset would cost her. She hated to replace the one she'd left behind as it was one of her favorites. If she was lucky, maybe someone at Baker Street had found it up in the Baskerville room and would return it to her armoire in the submissives' salon. She'd need a new thong, but that was far more affordable than a new custom or even semi-custom corset.

From one of the conference rooms on the upper floor of the internationally renowned Lloyd's building, the lone figure watched.

Text Message:020 5555 4321
Donovan leaving early and on her way home
Sister dealt with. We are good to go

CHAPTER 7

Rhys ducked into one of the corset shops that offered custom and semi-custom items. It was where she'd bought the lilac corset. Nothing really tickled her fancy and as she was browsing, she found herself feeling light-headed. Maybe Laura was right; perhaps she was coming down with something.

Darting across the street to the tube station, Rhys jumped on a train and exited close to her flat. Her place wasn't big, but she'd opted for location and high-end amenities over space. After all, it was just her, and she wasn't planning for that to change any time soon. Opening the door, she looked around. Everything seemed like it was in place, but the hairs on the back of her neck stood up. Why did something feel off?

She walked through the flat, which didn't take

long. It occupied the small top floor of an Edwardian townhouse facing the Thames. It had tall ceilings and large windows, giving the space a light and airy feeling. It was mainly two big rooms with one functioning as her living room, kitchen and office area and the other serving as a large bedroom and attached bath. The bedroom had a set of large French doors leading into it. She always kept the doors open so the bed could be seen from the main room.

Feeling foolish for her skittishness, Rhys checked the bath and bedroom before returning to the main room, but there was still something making her skin prickle. Something was off. Thinking about her neck, she reached beneath her hair and felt the puncture wounds—one on either side of the nape of her neck. Hurrying back to the bath, she lifted her hair with one hand and used the other to hold a hand mirror to look at the back of her neck, which was reflected in the wall mirror. What the hell? Those were absolutely puncture marks, and if she didn't know better, she'd think they were from some kind of large predator as they very much resembled a bite mark.

The on again/off again feeling of dizziness swept over her and she turned so she could grasp the vanity to steady herself. This time a wave of nausea accompanied the vertigo. When she closed her eyes to stop the room from spinning, she had a vague memory of the first time Lars had taken her from behind and cringed, remembering the searing pain in her neck.

The sonofabitch *had* bitten her. But what kind of human could inflict such a bite? Too much space between the puncture wounds to be a vampire—even if she believed in such things, which she didn't.

Taking a deep breath, she steadied herself and started back to the sitting area. She stopped, looking at the door to the walk-in closet and debated with herself about whether she should open it to check for hobgoblins hiding within. Rhys tried to convince herself that opening the door and checking her closet was foolishness. The little voice inside her head said 'who cares? No one will know.' She decided the little voice was right.

She crossed to her bed and quietly, in case someone was waiting for her, slipped her hand into her nightstand and wrapped it around her pepper spray. The stuff was illegal as all get out in the UK, but Maeve had brought it to her. Rhys never took it out of her flat, but it did make her feel better knowing it was there in her bedroom. She moved casually around to the other side of the bed as if to look out the window.

A slight movement caught her eye. Had she actually seen someone duck behind a large lorry parked just down from her flat? Surely not. Nonetheless, she pulled the shade and turned on the light beside the bed, dropping down quickly to check under the bed before rushing to the closet. She threw open the door and turned on the light, her pepper spray at the ready.

Feeling silly, because of course no one was there, she sighed and chalked it up to her increasing sense of malaise.

Rhys tossed the pepper spray back onto her bed, shook her head at the paranoia she was experiencing, and exited into the main room. Grateful for her Tovala smart oven and the prepared meal in her fridge, she scanned the barcode for fish tacos, put it in the oven, and hit start. She walked to the fridge, grabbed an Otter Ale, and sat down at her desk, opening her laptop so she could start her memo to her boss about the Raphael.

The oven dinged and she went to get her food. She knew that all the advertisements for it showed people sitting down with the food displayed beautifully on the plate. She was pretty sure most people ate it out of the container, just like her. Coming back with her food and a fork she noticed the laptop was booted up. She stopped midway between the kitchen island and her desk. She didn't remember turning it on just now and knew for a fact she'd turned it off before she'd gone to Baker Street the night before.

Again, that prickly feeling of something not quite right crawled up her spine. Setting her food back on the kitchen counter, she walked into her bedroom, picked up the pepper spray and did an even more thorough search than she had before, including moving around the clothing in her walk-in closet. Ignoring the little voice that kept whispering she needed to get out of her flat, she took her trusty, totally illegal pepper spray back into the main room, picking up her dinner along the way.

She sat down at her desk, went through her email, browsed her social media as well as Maeve's, and then settled down to write the memo. The fish tacos and beer might not have been the dinner most people who weren't feeling well would have chosen, but it was one of her favorites. She stared at her email. Nothing from Maeve since her last message two days before they were supposed to meet in Vienna.

Where are you, Maeve?

From the time Maeve failed to show, she'd gotten the run around from Interpol's headquarters in Lyon and the satellite office in Stockholm. She felt tears forming in her eyes. Before this, she'd been pissed. First, at Maeve for not meeting her in Vienna, and then at the seeming indifference for her concern for her sister's safety from her employer, who wouldn't even admit they were Maeve's employer.

She was still convinced that Lars Jakobsson was involved and had more than likely done something to her sister. Her great plan to seduce and get him to tell her everything had, in retrospect, been both stupid and ill-conceived. There was something inherently flawed in believing she could use her own submissive nature to somehow fool him into giving her what she needed to convict him. Regardless, she had been completely and utterly unsuccessful. The man was a gangster, ran Sweden's largest syndicate and was reputed to be part of a powerful coalition with two other major organized crime syndicates.

What had she been thinking? And where was her sister?

Shaking her head as if she could shake off her worries, concerns, and fears about her sister, Rhys turned to her computer and began to write the email, outlining for her boss her concerns about the Raphael. The craquelure was the only thing she could really hang her hat on, but combined with the iffy visual style and provenance, she didn't feel that they, or at least she, could attest to the authenticity of the painting. That didn't mean some other art expert wouldn't but when it was revealed to be a fake, and they almost always were, Lloyds wouldn't be on the hook for it.

Summary of her work, tests, analysis, and recommendations done, Rhys saved the email in her drafts folder so she could review it in the morning before hitting send. As lousy as she was feeling, she wanted to make sure it was clear, concise, and communicated what she wanted.

Rhys stared at her computer screen. Knowing it was a bad idea, she went ahead and did a search on her browser for Lars Jakobsson. Considering what she knew about him, there wasn't really a lot to be found. There was quite a bit about his home, Runestone, and his heritage. But not so much as a hint that he was a mobster or even a smuggler. She wondered if he paid someone to ensure the stories he wanted out on the net stayed at the top of any search results.

Rhys then searched for her sister, both with her real name and with her false identity, Mara Donahue. Nothing. It was as if her sister had disappeared off the face of the earth and that only Rhys was left to wonder how and why.

Her work done, Rhys stood and stretched. She couldn't resist going back to the window and looking down onto the street below. The van was still there, but this time there was no movement to catch her eye. It must have just been a bit of nothing that her feeling bad embellished with sinister character. She cleaned up from dinner, which consisted of tossing the food container and her beer bottle in the rubbish, wiping down the oven, and washing the fork. She grabbed another beer and headed into her sitting room to put her feet up and watched a ballet DVD of *Swan Lake* she had recently purchased. She allowed the beauty of the music and the dancing to sweep her away.

The sun had gone down and the entire flat was shrouded in darkness when she heard the squeak of the floorboard right outside her bedroom doors. The first time Maeve had visited the flat, she'd told Rhys not to fix it as it would always alert her that someone was there. She realized she was hidden behind the arm of the couch and quietly peeked over it, catching her breath and bringing her hand up to cover her mouth.

Two men, all in black, were entering her bedroom. What should she do? Stay put and hope they didn't want to steal her television and DVR? If they did, they would surely see her, just as they would if they went to steal her laptop and turned towards the door. They were rummaging around in her bedroom.

One of them snickered on her side of the bed and she felt herself turn beet red. She was fairly sure the guy had just discovered her vibrator. She could see the headlines now *"Trusted Art Expert for Lloyd's Found Murdered Next to Sex Toy!"* One of them had moved into the bath while the one who'd discovered her 'little friend' moved into her walk-in closet. What were they looking for?

As one of them came back towards the main room, he stepped on the creaking board and Rhys slipped down behind the arm of the sofa, trying to make herself as small and unobtrusive as possible. The problem became that, even if they couldn't see her, she would have no advance knowledge of them seeing her before it was too late.

Too late for what? Did she suddenly think she could attack two good-sized men with less than honorable intent? Had she suddenly become some kind of ninja? Perhaps she could leap the back of her couch and run out the front door. Two problems: behind her couch there was a wall, and her lock had a deadbolt that she was pretty sure she'd locked. Maybe they would just go away. They had shown no interest in her jewelry or the Tovala. They had looked on her computer but hadn't unplugged it or the printer. What the hell were they after?

She was sure she could hear them turning as if they were going to leave. Perhaps whatever they'd come for they'd either found and had it with them or had decided it wasn't here. Rhys was just beginning to believe she might make it out of her flat without incident. She would ensure the door was double locked, wedge one of the kitchen chairs under the door handle and call Scotland Yard.

But what would she tell the Yard? Two men, that she couldn't identify, had broken into her flat and mooched around before leaving? Maybe she'd save that last part until after they came. In the interim she would go where she thought they had been to see if there was anything missing.

Just when she was about to believe she would be okay, she heard. "Well, well, well. Lookie here, Artie. If it ain't the little lady herself. I told you she had to be here somewhere."

"Guess you were right. When we finish the job, I owe you a beer."

"Finish?" she squeaked.

"Yeah, your sister was a very naughty girl. It

seems no one can find her. The boss thinks if he has you, maybe she'll come out of hiding."

"Don't give us no trouble. You be a good girl and show us a little affection," he said suggestively cupping his crotch, "and maybe we'll let you ride in the back seat."

Rhys shook her head. "No. What do you want with me?"

"That's none of your business," said Artie. "You're coming with us. You better know how to get hold of your sister or you can kiss this flat and your life goodbye."

The two goons advanced on her. Rhys thought there was a very good chance that she was not going to make it out of this alive after all. She thought she'd always heard your life was supposed to pass before your eyes in a situation such as this, but she didn't see her deceased parents or Maeve. Didn't see their childhood home or any of the fun times she'd had.

The thing that filled her mind was Lars Jakobsson, his home in Sweden, and tigers… white tigers, lots of them. The vision was replaced by a silvery cloud that whirled all around her, crackling with electricity and flashing the brilliant colors of the Aurora Borealis in front of her eyes. Rhys thought about the fact that she'd always wanted to see the Northern Lights in person. She thought they had a certain kind of magick, and it was said that if one knew their secrets, they could reach across time and space to see the past and the future.

One of the white tigers seemed to train its violet eyes on her. The sleek, predatory cat roared and charged toward her, leaping as if to take her down. Rhys cried out, putting her hands in front of her face as if to ward it or the two brigands in her home away —only the sound came out as a roar!

CHAPTER 8

Rhys' two assailants screamed in fear, holding up their arms as if to hold her off and trying to scramble away. Her instinct was to pursue them, take them down and rip their throats out. Rhys fought that imperative and turned to the large window, rushing towards it and crashing through it out onto the roof, splintering glass and framing everywhere. She could feel and hear the crunching of the glass beneath her feet, but there was no pain.

Holy shit! There was shattered glass everywhere, including under her feet—all four of them! Looking down, Rhys was overwhelmed, almost losing her footing on the slippery roof as she saw two large white paws with black stripes. She could feel the different textures of the slate roof as something within her compelled her to run along the spine of the roof toward the next building, leaping the space between them as if it were nothing. She landed, sure footed, and galloped toward the edge of the house she was on, away from the light.

The house at the end of the block had a tiered roof and when she'd landed on it, she turned and did a controlled slide down until she could leap to the ground. It was still a long way down and she expected it to hurt, but it didn't. Her front paws—hands—limbs—hit the grass and started to move as she heard two more footfalls and glanced back over her shoulder only to realize it was her hind end... and there was a tail.

She was the tiger, or the tiger was her, or she was asleep, and this was a really bizarre dream, or the two thugs had given her drugs and she was taking a really bad trip. Rhys had heard that it only took once for LSD to really mess with your mind. She looked back down the road in the direction of the flat and saw the suspicious van she'd seen earlier pull away from the curb. So, she had been right to be concerned.

Who were they? What did they want? And what the hell happened to me?

Jumping the barrier, she charged through the bushes, noticing the thorns, but not really feeling any pain from them. She made her way down to the hard packed path that ran along the side of the Thames. At this time of night, the walkways were mostly deserted, but the few individuals who were out and spotted her, reached for their mobile phones, for sure calling emergency services while taking video of her.

Must run! Must hide! Must find Lars!

The imperatives tumbled through her mind chaotically as she tried to figure out what the hell she was going to do. She didn't understand any of this. This, she reminded herself, had to be either a dream or a bad acid trip. People didn't just transform into wild animals, no matter how rare and beautiful they might be.

"Rhys! Rhys!" she heard him shout.

She skidded to a halt and looked back toward the sound.

"Rhys!" Lars called again. *'I'm here, Skönhet. Stay where you are. Get off the path and into the bushes. Do not be afraid. Listen to your tigress. She will protect you. I'm coming.'*

She could hear him as clear as a bell, but it wasn't because he was shouting or calling to her. The comforting sound of his voice filled her mind and brought her the same kind of peace Lars had the night before when he'd made a sound that closely resembled a purr. A purr? Had it been an actual purr? Why was—what did he call this beast whose mind, body, and spirit she seemed entwined with?—her tigress so insistent that she do as he commanded?

Fuck! How did she get the only tigress in history

that wanted to be submissive? Tigers, especially the rare white ones, had always fascinated her. She knew that in the wild, tigers lived alone. They only came together as adults to mate, with the male leaving shortly after breeding was done. The female then raised her cubs alone.

Lars called again, this time the voice inside her head was angry. *"I told you to hide in the bushes; do it now!"* and instead of a purr, there was a growl.

Fuck him! Both she and the tigress agreed he had no right to talk to her that way, especially with everything that was happening to her. She could feel the anger and resentment in the tigress. Her ears flattened and her tail moved back and forth slowly, the tip flipping in an agitated manner. She made a hissing, muffled roar, showing her teeth with her hackles raised. Well, at least they were in agreement.

The sounds of blaring sirens could be heard getting closer. Apparently, someone had been able to make the police believe there was a tiger on the loose. Time to put some distance between her, the cops, the goons, and Lars Jakobsson. Instead of turning toward the bushes, she whirled on her hind feet and bounded towards the embankment. The Thames at this location was less than half a mile wide and there were more places to hide on the other side.

As she rushed towards the edge, she gathered herself, springing and pushing off with her back feet, clearing the railing easily and plunging into the icy water. Hmm, it wasn't too bad with all this fur. Fur? She couldn't have fur, and yet she did. She moved powerfully through the dark water, making the crossing in approximately fifteen minutes. She kept her eyes on the opposite bank and found a deserted stretch with heavy foliage. It looked like a good place to climb out of the water, rest, and dry off. She had no idea what the hell she was going to do as a tiger in London.

～

They had her address and were en route to Rhys' flat. One of the other SUVs had joined him and the other two should be here shortly. They drove past the house that contained her flat and Lars noticed the suspicious van parked across the street.

"We're going to pull into the space between the two houses," said Lars into his communicator. "The rest of you go behind the back."

"Did you see the van Alpha?"

"I did. If one of you who isn't with us could get out of the SUV a ways back and casually walk by the van to see if there is anyone in there we need to worry about, that would be helpful. Take a picture of the plates, although I suspect they're stolen."

"I'll do it, Lars."

"Good. Find a spot to park where you won't be seen and wait for my instructions."

"How do you want to handle this?" asked his driver.

"If possible, I'd like to slip up to her flat, break in, bind and gag her, and then get out of London. The sooner we're on our way home to Runestone, the better I'll like it."

"You'd best take someone with you in case whoever is in that van is not feeling kindly towards your mate. If you can come out through the back garden, it will cut down on the likelihood of being seen."

Lars nodded, unbuckling his seatbelt as the SUV glided to a stop. "Heads up. Here we go."

As he exited the vehicle, he looked up to see a beautiful white tigress leaping from Rhys' building to the house next door. Damn it. The transmutation was complete.

"Some of you cover that van and the others go into her building. Go up to her flat and get it closed up. Check for bodies," growled Lars.

"Alpha?"

"Apparently my mate was threatened, and her tigress has taken over. We're going to follow her and see if we can't get her calm enough to shift, get her in the SUV and then get to the plane."

Lars jumped back into the SUV, and they pulled off, driving down the road. Lars kept his eyes on his mate as she made her way over the rooftops of several houses, shunning the light, before getting to the house on the end where she made her way down the roof and jumped onto the ground. He could only imagine the fear and questions his mate had to have regarding what was happening to her. Of course, he reminded himself, if she had remained in their bed, none of this would be happening. Watching her move, it seemed as if Rhys had accepted her tigress or else the tigress had just completely overwhelmed her.

He tried to reach out to her through the bonding link. It was as if he could hear her thoughts and feel her emotions, but any attempts to pacify her were rejected as the tigress roared down the link at the intruder.

He watched as a white flash streaked across the street and bounded down the path that bordered the Thames. "Follow her," growled Lars and then taking a deep breath, continued, "apologies."

"None are necessary, Alpha. Your concern for your mate is understandable, and she does not appear to hear you."

"Oh, she hears me all right. Her tigress is pissed and determined to keep her other half safe. Get me close and I'll see if I can't catch up with her."

"She won't get away from us."

They drove parallel to Rhys' path and watched as she rushed past the few people who were out, surprising them as she galloped past. No wonder. It wasn't every day there was a white tiger on the loose, running around the streets of London.

The SUV had barely come to a stop before Lars was out and running down the steps from the street level to get to the path level. When he spotted her, he shouted, "Rhys! Rhys!"

She skidded to a halt and looked back toward him. If tigress and human were coming together to share themselves one with the other, Rhys was going to prove a formidable opponent. She had been born and raised in London. This was her home, and she knew it far better than he. With her knowledge of the city and the power of her tigress, she would be difficult to capture and get home to the safety of Runestone.

He tapped the communication bud in his ear. The new technology didn't require it, but old habits were hard to break. "Anything from Rhys' flat?"

"No, Alpha, there's no one here. Her tigress must have gone through the window."

Lars heard gunshots—not what he wanted to hear. "Report."

"They got away, Alpha. They surprised us and started shooting. We had to dive for cover."

"Everyone all right?"

"One slight graze. But it's barely bleeding."

"Those in her flat—grab her things and then get out of there. Jonas and I will try and find my mate. Oskar and Leif, get around to the embankment on the other side of the Thames. The rest of you, get back to the plane and be ready to go. I have a helicopter on standby. We'll join you as soon as we can."

He could hear sirens in the distance. "Move," said Lars. "We need to avoid any entanglements with the authorities."

He turned back to the path and spotted her. "Rhys!" he called out loud again. Trying to reach her along the tether, he verbalized in his mind. *I'm here, Skönhet. Stay where you are. Get off the path and into the bushes. Do not be afraid. Listen to your tigress. She will protect you. I'm coming.*

He didn't wait for her response but started running toward her position. Her response, when it came, was neither welcome nor unexpected. Rhys was bonding with her tigress and right now, neither was feeling kindly towards him. On the best of days, tigresses needed to be handled with a firm, but deft hand. When angered, frightened, or confused they tended to bite and scratch first and listen to explanations later—usually when pinned down across a tiger's lap getting their backsides blistered.

Lars swore under his breath. He'd done himself no favors when he'd chosen to give her a pass on the discipline he should have administered the night before. When he had her safely back in his arms, he meant to correct that mistake and then he would answer all her questions.

Her response was to growl, hiss, and show her

teeth before whirling away, charging down the hill and diving into the icy water of the Thames. With mobile phones and cameras clicking away, Lars had no choice but to let her go. He couldn't very well shift and run her down, however much he might want to.

CHAPTER 9

Surprisingly the bushes on this side of the river held no thorns and were actually comforting as they folded her into their embrace. Rhys felt safe and hidden. She could see Lars on the other side of the Thames, surrounded by gawking onlookers. No doubt he'd seen her plunge into the water, and most likely noted where she got out. She was no longer safe; she needed to find a place to hide and to figure out what to do next.

Crawling out from beneath the bushes, she shook herself and, keeping to the shadows, loped towards the docks. She should be able to find help there—well, maybe not help, but at least a safe place to hide until she could figure out her next move. Oddly, she wasn't afraid. The presence of the tigress calmed her.

While she was grateful to whatever had given her the ability to shift into a tigress, she couldn't go running around London as one. Besides she hadn't grabbed any of the things she would need to find a more conventional way of hiding. There were some that even if she had them, she probably didn't want to use—credit cards, mobile phone, etc. One thing Maeve had taught her, though, was to have her passport, some cash, and some credit cards she didn't normally use stored in a bank that wasn't her regular one.

At the time, Rhys had thought it was a game, but she was beginning to understand having fun had nothing to do with it. Had Maeve wanted to prepare her in case something went very wrong—something like what had happened tonight? What had happened? Who were those men? Who was their boss and what did he want with her? Did they work for Lars? No, that didn't feel right. Something told her that whatever those men had planned, they hadn't been ordered to do so by the head of the Berserker Syndicate. She wasn't sure how she knew, but she did. She had not just sensed, but felt, his anxiety over her safety and then his anger when she had hissed at him. She grinned. Feeling him taken aback at her defiance was the highlight of this whole thing—well, that and not getting raped, killed, or both.

Besides, where did he get off being angry? Whatever the hell was going on with her, she was pretty damn sure Lars Jakobsson was the cause of it. He hadn't seemed at all surprised that somehow, she was a white tiger. Somehow, he had known he could reach across some link that seemed to exist between them and communicate with her. This side of the Thames was practically deserted, but she had no doubt in her mind that Lars was coming. He would not give up. Most likely he would have men with him—men who would do whatever their don asked of them. If he'd seen her jump into the river, he would have dispatched them to this side to look for her.

The tigress with whom she now, inexplicably, shared a mind, spirit, and body was restless and wanted to move. Rhys allowed her free rein and they —she—it… galloped off into the night, instinctively putting distance between herself and those who sought to capture her. At this point she didn't know who to trust except herself, and luckily that included her tigress.

The night air rippled across her wet fur, drying it as they ran. The bank where she had her—what was it Maeve had called it? Right, a *go* bag—was on the other side of the Thames. If she could find a phone to use, she might be able to get the bank to send a car for her. She needed to find a place to get off the street and hide. But how did one hide a white tiger? She/It/They were considerably larger in this form, and unless she was mistaken, were larger than the tigers she had seen in captivity. She had once loved to go to the zoo and could watch the big cats for hours. Now, the idea of tigers being caged almost made her retch. She knew zoos had their place and did their best to nurture the animals in their care. In fact, she knew that many had been responsible for bringing several species back from the brink of extinction. That knowledge did little to assuage her tigress' revulsion.

Rhys looked up and saw an open window in what appeared to be a warehouse closed for the night. The window was up high, but she was certain she could scramble over the chain link fence and make her way up to the opening. Having the strength of her tigress to call on, she sprang to the top of the fence, landing lightly on the other side. As her feet reached the ground, barking dogs sounded the alarm as they ran towards her position. Normally she would be concerned, but she was pretty damn sure in a confrontation between two dogs and a tiger, the tiger won.

Two rottweilers rounded the corner of the building, snarling and snapping until they skidded to a halt. Apparently, they hadn't been expecting to be outclassed in weight, size, and lethal ability. She hissed at them, showing her teeth and crouching. Both dogs tucked tail and ran like hell. Well, that was kind of fun. She could hear the tigress making a chuffing sound, which felt very much like laughter.

Rhys loped along the perimeter of the building until she found a large rubbish dumpster. She leaped on top of it and then onto the lower portion of the roof, trotting up the sloping structure until she reached the spine, which was easily traversed with a front and back leg on either side. She reached the broken window. Not big enough for her tigress.

Rhys realized the tigress had taken over when they'd been threatened. It was going to be easier if she just thought of them as a dual entity. *So how do I make you go away? And if you do? How do I get you back?*

'I am always with you,' she heard the tigress answer. *'We are one. You are in control unless I am needed. Ask me to leave and I shall, but I will always be just at the fringes of your mind. When you need or want me, just call to me, and I will be there.'*

"Thank you," Rhys whispered. "You saved my/our life. But we're going to do better if I take over now."

She could see the tigress nod in her mind and felt the warmth of the swirling silver mist with the electrical bolts and kaleidoscope of colors envelop her as she became human again. Rhys had to admit the sensation was not unpleasant and left her aroused, hungry, and exhausted. She could feel the cool evening breeze as it slid across her skin. Her nipples beaded in response and Rhys looked down, only to discover she was naked—that was going to be a problem.

Rhys was able to crawl through the broken portion of the window without cutting herself. Once inside, she closed her eyes and called to the tigress.

Until she found clothes, she was probably, at least for now, safer as the tigress. She felt the tigress rush to the fore as the swirl of silver and color whirled all around her and she felt the change wash over her.

She crouched down, listening. The tigress' sense of hearing, smell, and night vision were far superior to her human ones. Sensing nothing to concern them, the tigress trotted around the third floor and then down the stairs to the second. As she explored the second floor, which seemed to have locker rooms and offices, she noticed a set of headlights a split second before the rottweilers did.

Rhys could feel Lars probing at her mind. Could he sense they were within? *'Yes,'* answered the tigress. She could feel the tigress closing down whatever psychic link existed between her and Lars. She sent her apologies to her tigress for ever thinking her submissive. She hid in the shadows until the SUV pulled away.

Nothing on this floor, or at least nothing she wanted to put on if she could help it. Finally, on the first floor, she found a delivery of clean uniforms. Not fashionable, but they would do. She bade her tigress to retreat and was once more human. She pulled on the smallest set of coveralls, which didn't fit her too badly. They had passed a pallet of imported trainers. Rhys retraced her steps, finding them and searching for her size. Slipping them on she sighed. At least now she was clothed, and her feet were protected.

There had been an employee lounge with a refrigerator. Looking inside she snagged two people's lunch. She tore off the names on the containers, vowing to herself to send them something to replace what she was eating. Rhys was ravenous and exhausted; apparently this shifting thing took a lot out of a girl. She was horny too. But the thought of anyone other than Lars touching her, including herself, was repugnant.

Rhys made her way back up to the third floor. If she remembered correctly, she'd seen a couch that looked relatively clean. She scavenged some blankets and made her way to her makeshift bed. Stretching out, she yawned. It wasn't too bad. She made herself as comfortable as possible.

Her first stop in the morning would be the Canadian Imperial Bank located in Cheapside. The question was, how to get there? At Maeve's insistence, Rhys had set it up so that if she were in just this situation, she could access her safety deposit box with a series of passwords and a thumbprint. The bank opened at eleven.

Nothing left to do but hunker down and wait for morning.

~

They searched all night to no avail. Lars thought he'd felt an inkling of her presence at one warehouse but the angry rottweilers convinced him it was best to wait until morning. He knew that as his tiger he could take the two dogs in a fight, but it wouldn't be a fair fight and it wasn't their fault they were caught up in something outside their experience when they were just trying to do their job.

The tentative probe along the tether had been shut down. He no longer believed the tigress was in control. Rather, he believed the two spirits had bonded and were now working together. Rhys wouldn't know about the bonding link, much less how to shut it down on her end, but the tigress would. He and his tiger would have words with Rhys and her tigress when they were reunited. He would communicate to her that such behavior was unwarranted and unsafe and would earn her a discipline session over his knee.

"Alpha?" said Jonas.

Lars snapped his head around. "Send the others back to the airport. They can sleep there. You and I will find a hotel close to her flat. She has no clothes, no money, no passport. She will have to return there or send someone to do it for her."

Once he'd secured two rooms in a small, sleek boutique hotel. Lars took a shower and then called Björn.

"I've heard from the others," he answered without preamble. "Should I send more men?"

"It isn't a question of more men; it's a question of figuring out her next move before she does and then being in place to intercept her and get her to safety."

"You sound far less anxious than I would be," said Björn.

Lars laughed. "You didn't see her, Björn. She was magnificent. The Gift must have taken hold quickly and she had to have embraced her tigress for them to move like that. Jumping rooftops, down riverbanks and into the Thames. She eluded those who sought to abduct her and all of us. I think I know where she may be, but I don't know for sure, and I'd bet money that she won't be there come morning."

"Your mate sounds like a worthy opponent," said Björn, amusement present in his voice.

"I would rather she was my bedmate, which she will be as soon as I get my hands on her."

"Britt wants me to remind you that as you didn't have a chance to explain things, she is probably frightened."

Lars laughed. "You tell Britt, I wish that's what I felt coming down the tether. My mate might be confused, although I suspect that is dissipating and being quickly replaced by anger and understanding. When I called to her and commanded that she stop, she growled and hissed at me, flattening her ears and showing me her teeth. She has quite the temper, my mate, and little to no fear of me."

"Well, once she has felt your barbs, I imagine she

will yowl and hiss for another reason before she submits to your will and purrs for you."

Björn caught him up on other clan business and as Lars suspected, Björn had it all under control. His lifelong friend had proved, over the years, to be an exceptional beta.

"Any more news on Maeve?" asked Lars.

"Still nothing. I did hear from our man at Interpol. They are growing more concerned by the day. She has not reported in, and rumor has it that members of both sides of those who were at the exchange site are looking for her."

"Have you explained to them that we are still willing and able to broker the deal?"

"Yes, Alpha. I even offered to give up our commission for their trouble if they would cease looking for the Interpol agent or anyone who was related to her. I didn't want to tip our hand that her sister was important to you, but I thought it important to try and get both Rhys and her sister out of their crosshairs."

"For what it's worth, I don't think we were successful. Someone tried to kidnap my mate this evening." Lars chuckled. "From the looks of it, they met her tigress. That alone is problematic. We need to find those men and dispose of them. They could betray our secret. Go ahead and inform both sides of the conflict that if I find someone is trying to visit retribution on Maeve or anyone close to her, my revenge will be swift and brutal. Tell them I do not want Interpol looking to put our head on spikes outside Runestone's walls."

"Yes, Alpha."

After he ended the call, he prowled around the room, finally going to stand on the small balcony outside his room, overlooking the Thames.

"Where are you Rhys?" he whispered to the wind. "Hear me, my mate, you are mine. I have claimed you in the ancient way of our kind and your destiny is now intertwined with mine. Stay safe this night, for tomorrow I will find you and take you home."

He turned to go back into his room. From somewhere across the river, he heard a gentle chuffing coming down the link.

'Catch me if you can, my alpha, for we will not be subject to the whims of man nor tiger.'

Lars smiled. Rhys was safe and most likely asleep, but the tigress watched over her. She might well lead him on a wild goose chase, but in the end, all would be well, and Rhys would learn to embrace her new life and the pair of them would be brought to heel.

CHAPTER 10

The sounds of the warehouse district coming to life disturbed Rhys' restless slumber. She listened intently and couldn't hear anything inside the building she was in. Quietly, she made her way downstairs to see if she couldn't get her hands on some cash. Riffling through the pockets of several jackets and some desk drawers, she came up with a whopping forty pounds. Not a great deal to be sure, but enough to scrounge a breakfast from one of the food trucks and get her a ride to the Canadian Imperial Bank. She meant to be there when they opened.

Rhys hated the idea of stealing but she had no other recourse but to do so. She grabbed a business card from the desk so she could return the money down the line. She found a working phone and placed a call to her office, leaving a message that she was not feeling well and would most likely not be in until the following Monday. The second call was to engage a for-hire transport. Slinking along the front of the warehouse, she looked out to see the front gate open and a worker was leashing up the guard dogs. She slipped out of the warehouse and walked briskly to the street beyond the gate just as her ride pulled up.

After having the driver take her to one of the large hotels, she waited for him to leave and then caught a bus to one of her favorite street food vendors and purchased a breakfast burrito bowl and cup of espresso. As she took her first bite, she wasn't sure if anything had ever tasted better. Once she was finished, she adjourned to the central courtyard outside the tube station. Shortly before the bank opened, Rhys trotted down the stairs to the underground, hopped on a car and emerged at the stop a short walk from the bank. At each stage, she scanned the area around her to ensure she wasn't being followed. She didn't have the same hair standing up on the back of her neck feeling as she had yesterday, but it never hurt to be overly cautious.

She arrived shortly after the bank opened and walked to the customer service desk and asked to see the head of the security deposit box department.

A tall, thin man with a crooked aquiline nose, dressed in an impeccable dark gray suit approached. "Ms. Donovan? My name is Reginald Dwight, how may I be of service?" His tone was respectful, but the way he glanced over her coveralls and trainers said he wasn't impressed.

"I have a safety deposit box here with special instructions for allowing me to access it," she replied coolly.

He nodded and gestured towards the safety deposit box area. "This way, Ms. Donovan." He led Rhys back to a secure room, just outside the safe where the secure boxes were kept. He had her scan both her fingerprint and her iris. "Codeword?"

Maeve had suggested she use a word no one would associate with her and offered that she had used the name of her favorite stuffed animal from their childhood. She looked Mr. Dwight in the eye, smiled sweetly and said, "Tigger." The irony of it with her current state did not escape her.

Dwight led her into the safe itself and into a privacy room where he brought her the box, which had an electronic combination lock to open the box itself.

"If you need further assistance, I will be right outside."

"Thank you, Mr. Dwight, I won't be but a minute."

Opening the box, she was grateful for the deep pockets of the coverall. She should be able to discreetly conceal the contents of the box—duplicates of her passport and driver's license, unused credit cards, a good deal of cash and a pay-as-you-go-mobile phone. She ducked out of the room, bid Mr. Dwight *adieu*, and made her way back to the underground, changing trains and taking a circuitous route before arriving at the Eurostar train station where she purchased a ticket for the bullet train to Paris. Once in Paris, she purchased clothing—bra, leggings, Ugg boots, a sweater, jacket, knit hat, and a small crossbody bag. Nothing particularly fashionable. She wanted to blend in with locals once she was outside Paris. The vendor with the water-repellant jacket also sold pepper spray and she purchased two—one for her coat pocket and one for her bag. Unlike in London, pepper spray was legal in Paris.

Tucking her hair under the cap and keeping her head down, she made her way to one of the rental agencies where she rented a car and drove south to Lyon where her sister's real flat for her real life was located. She looped through and around Paris, ensuring no one was following her, before heading to Lyon. Several times she got off the freeway, driving out of sight to ensure she wasn't being followed. Finally, she drove to her sister's flat and was relieved to see Maeve's car parked in its designated spot. Pulling into one of the guest slots, Rhys ran inside the building and up to her sister's place.

She knocked on the door and when there was no answer, she used the key she had left in the safety deposit box and let herself inside, calling her sister's name and receiving no response. She locked the door behind her and reached into her pocket, pulling out the pepper spray, ready to defend herself as she searched her sister's flat. After going through everything, she was convinced neither Maeve nor anyone else had been through the flat since the last time Rhys had done so.

Where are you, Maeve? Why is your car downstairs? It hadn't been the last time Rhys had been here. When Maeve had failed to show in Vienna, Rhys had come to Lyon. She hadn't found her that time, either.

Rhys walked to the window, not pulling the curtain out of her way until she had looked long and hard both up and down the street. Nothing. It was a quiet little street. Rhys peeked out the window, pulling back the drape from the casing to stare at the river below. The knock on the door was unexpected and made her jump back, readying her pepper spray. She would try that first, but if that was ineffective, she could feel her tigress at the ready.

A louder knocking came, followed by, "*Police Nationale*" His tone was loud, but didn't sound angry, more like he was trying to be heard through a thick door.

She crossed to the door, looking out the peephole to find two uniformed officers of the *gendarmes*. They looked legit, but then she was no expert. But would imposters be making the row they were? Pocketing the pepper spray, she cracked open the door.

"Hi, officers. Can I help you? I'm sorry. I don't

speak French, and my sister doesn't seem to be home." Rhys said, trying to act as neutral and calm as she could even though her heart was beating in her chest and her tigress prowled at the fringes of her mind, growling.

"That is all right... is it Ms. Donovan?" the younger of the two officers said in perfect, heavily accented English.

Rhys gave them a big smile, opened the door and ushered them in. "Yes, it is."

"Might I see some identification?"

"Uhm, sure," Rhys said, opening her bag and handing him her driver's license. He looked at the name and back up at her face as if double checking it was her face on the license. "I was supposed to meet my sister in Vienna for a little break, but she never showed. I came back here, hoping to find her. I saw her car downstairs, but as you can see, Maeve's not here," she said, glancing around the flat.

The two *gendarmes* looked back and forth between themselves. Rhys was starting to have a really bad feeling about all of this. She had figured Maeve was missing, but as she hadn't reported it, why would the cops be here?

"Can I ask what business you have with my sister?"

"One of the neighbors saw you entering your sister's apartment and called it in," answered the younger officer.

"I have her key," said Rhys, holding it up. "And you've confirmed that I am who I say I am. Why would the neighbor call it in?"

Again, the two officers looked at each other before looking at her.

"Has something happened to my sister?" she asked, as dread began to pool in her gut. She could think of no good reason this scenario would be playing out this way.

"I'm afraid we need you to come down to the morgue," the one officer said gently.

"No," Rhys said, shaking her head and backing away. "Please, no."

"I am so sorry, but we need someone to make a definitive identification of the body, and as next of kin, I'm afraid that job belongs to you."

She nodded woodenly, tears filling her eyes. Somewhere inside her mind, her tigress curled around her soul, offering her strength and understanding. How could this be true? Maeve couldn't be dead. Her light had always shone so brightly. How could it be dimmed forever? She shivered as cold shrouded her heart.

Rhys stood, the shivering becoming shaking as she tried to comprehend all the ramifications of his words. Maeve was dead. Someone was responsible, and that someone would pay. She didn't want to even glance at the mirror Maeve had always kept by the door. She had felt the color drain from her face and her throat threatened to close as she tried to force down the unshed tears.

"I am so sorry, Mademoiselle Donovan. We can drive you down and bring you back if you like."

He was trying to be so polite, so caring, when all she wanted to do was pummel him until he admitted that it was all some elaborate plot to make her believe Maeve was dead, but to what end?

"No. I'll lock up here and meet you there. I may be a few minutes here."

"If you like."

She made a last, thorough search, feeling under pieces of furniture and behind things hanging on the wall. Nothing. She looked in the toilet tank. Nothing. In the refrigerator. Nothing. Finally, she opened the door, paused to take a last look around, and walked away, closing the door behind her.

Rhys drove through the cold, rainy streets of Lyon, trying to figure out how this could be happening, and what her next move might be. She pulled up in front of the police station. She spotted a man standing casually against a streetlamp with a kind of studied nonchalance that could only be deliberate and cultivated. Rhys didn't care. She knew she had to get through this and knew her love for her sister would never let her not find those responsible and bring them to justice, but right now she had to focus on putting one foot in front of the other.

One of the policemen was waiting just inside the

door for her and accompanied her down to the morgue. It was a morgue like any other—no better, no worse. Although what she knew of morgues was from police procedurals and movies. This was her first time in a real one. She reached up to hug herself. Even with the sweater and lined waterproof jacket, she was cold and wondered if she'd ever be warm again.

CHAPTER 11

The technician opened the door to the drawer marked "Donovan, M." Rhys kept her distance. She didn't want to get any closer, but the policeman dragged her forward, the rubber soles of her boots skidding and catching on the polished cement floor. The drawer was open, and the technician grasped the lip along the underside of the table, pulling it out.

The technician reached for the sheet and began to draw it away from the face of the occupant. Rhys closed her eyes. *Please don't let it be Maeve. Please don't let it be Maeve.* But, of course, it was. She felt her knees begin to buckle. The cop prevented her from crumbling to the ground. She clung to him for the briefest moment, wondering where the hell Lars was and why he wasn't here with her. The thought was almost immediately pushed aside by the knowledge that he most likely was the one who'd put her sister on the slab.

"How…" she started. "How did she die?" she whispered, clutching at the cop's uniform as if it were a lifeline in a storm-tossed sea.

"We aren't sure. We will have to perform an autopsy to determine the cause of death. We are, however, treating her death as suspicious."

"Why?" she said, turning her tear-filled eyes on him. Anything not to have to look at Maeve.

"Is that your sister?" She nodded. "I need you to speak the words so the machines can record it."

"Yes," she croaked. "That's my sister, Maeve Donovan."

"She was found floating in the river. There was no obvious cause of death."

"Was she… was she raped?" she managed to get out.

"There were no signs of that, but it will be part of the autopsy."

"How long has she been dead?"

"Again, until the autopsy has been completed, we have no way of knowing."

Rhys couldn't force herself to move closer to the cold, lifeless body that had once been her sister.

"Do you know she worked for Interpol? Someone should call them and ask them what they know. Last I heard, she was investigating some mafia types in Stockholm."

"And yet you were meeting her in Vienna…"

The cop left the question dangling in the air and the hair on the back of her neck stood up as her tigress growled. Best to keep her answers short and sweet. "Yes. As I said, she didn't show so I came looking for her."

"I see," he said, but Rhys knew he didn't.

"I… I'd like to go now. I'm not feeling well…"

The tigress within her hissed, showing her teeth a moment before a large, warm hand wrapped around her upper arm. Still in the stupor from finding her sister dead, she only looked down at it. The hand belonged to Lars.

"Of course, you aren't feeling well, Rhys…"

So, he knew her name. Rhys wasn't sure if that was a good thing or not.

Lars leaned down to nuzzle her neck, whispering "They think either you killed her or know more than you do. I'm going to get you out of here. I'll take care of you. Tell your tigress to settle down." Rhys said nothing but nodded. Lars handed the cop his business card. Fleetingly she wondered what it said. Lars Jakobsson, Gangster? Mafia Don? Tiger-Shifter? "I'm going to take my fiancée now. If you have more questions, you can call."

"I am not sure we want Ms. Donovan leaving Lyon, let alone France," said the cop.

"We both know that's not up to you. You don't have enough to hold her, and don't think I won't be reporting the way you ambushed her this morning to your superiors. Shame on you. It is obvious my fiancée and her sister were close."

"If she is your fiancée, why isn't she wearing a ring?"

"We were going to look for one in Paris after she and her sister met in Vienna."

Lars didn't wait for a response from the *gendarme* before leading her away. She went quietly. For one thing, the vice-like grip on her arm precluded her pulling away. For another, Rhys was certain Lars could get her out of the morgue, Lyon, and France. She was convinced staying here was not in her best interest.

She turned back as the drawer with Maeve's body was pushed back into the bank of similar drawers. She wanted another minute. Just a moment alone with Maeve to say goodbye. But how could she say goodbye to the most alive person she'd ever known? How could Maeve be dead? Was the man trying to lead her out of the morgue responsible? If so, she would go with him and exact her revenge.

Rhys knew Interpol would not get justice for her sister. They'd proved that. They had already begun to disavow her sister's existence. Well, Maeve had lived. Someone had snuffed out her life and Rhys vowed to make them pay. If it wasn't Jakobsson, it was someone else. Regardless of who was responsible, Rhys vowed they would not get away with it.

"Come along, Rhys. The plane is waiting. Is there anything you need from Maeve's flat?"

"We have cordoned off the flat. No admittance," said the police officer.

She shook her head. "There's nothing there. I have a car…"

"That's all right. I'll have Leif gather your things and return the car." He turned to the cop. "We'll be at Visby on Gotland Island. The number is on my card. If you need anything from Rhys, she will be with me."

And with that he led her out the door. Was he really going to take her to Sweden, or would she just mysteriously disappear? Rhys realized at that precise moment, she didn't really care, but she had to keep herself alive because she knew down the road, she would care. The realization sparked life back into her. She would live, if for no other reason than to find Maeve's killer and make them pay.

Two men joined them as they walked to the waiting SUV. Lars reached into her coat pocket and pulled out the keys to her rental car. Thankfully, the pepper spray was in her other pocket.

"Leif, find Rhys' rental, collect her things and return the car. Then meet us at the plane. I need to get Rhys where they can't put their hands on her easily."

"Yes, Alpha," the hulk of a man said, taking the keys.

"Is everyone in your crime family almost as big as you?" she asked, looking up at Lars.

"Almost, but not quite," he said with a trace of humor. "I am sorry about your sister."

"Are you? Or do you just want me to believe you didn't kill her?"

A flash of anger, combined with sadness, came and went in his eyes. "If you truly believed that, you wouldn't have let me take you out of there, and the tigress inside you would be clamoring to get out."

"So, you know about that, do you?" Somehow it made perfect sense that he did. "What makes you think she isn't?"

"Because I can feel her calm resonating down the tether between us."

"Are you going to kill me?" she asked him.

"Of course not," the flash of anger was back. "I'm trying to get you out of here before the police here in Lyon or Interpol can keep you from leaving. At Runestone, we hold all the cards."

"Can't they ask for extradition?"

"Extradition is a slippery slope. If you'd been tried and convicted, it is fairly straightforward, but at this juncture of the case, the Swedish authorities would most likely allow you to stay with me."

"Because you own them?"

He chuckled softly. "No, sweetheart, because they have nothing to link you with your sister's death, and they would prefer not to have to deal with me."

"That's not overly reassuring."

Lars helped her into the SUV, getting in behind her. She could not only hear but feel the deep purring noise. 'Hear' was something of a misnomer as he was making no sound. But still it filled her with a sense of calm and reassurance.

The SUV pulled away from the building that housed both the morgue and the police station. Rhys wondered if maybe she should have put up a fuss when he'd taken her out of there, but she'd seen no other alternative. It had become obvious that the police suspected she either had a hand in killing her sister or at least knew more than she was saying, which was somewhat true.

"Stop doing that," she said, irritated. She didn't want to be soothed. She wanted to be angry. Anger might snap her out of this lethargy that seemed to have blanketed her so that she didn't feel like she could move.

"No. I can feel your upset. It is my responsibility to see you comforted."

"Did you kill my sister?" she asked again, this time watching him closely.

"Of course not. When I discovered your sister's real purpose in Stockholm, I fired her from my business there, but that is all I did. There was no reason for me to kill her, as her investigation had revealed nothing."

That made a certain kind of sense, especially since

Maeve had all but confirmed that her op had been blown, but that the subject of that mission had handled it with little rancor. Then, she'd invited Rhys to meet her in Vienna.

"The last time I talked to her, she was frustrated that she couldn't find anything to use against you. She said she knew the company and you were dirty as hell; she just couldn't prove it. She was rather vexed that she wasn't able to discover anything incriminating enough to break your organization and put you away. She didn't say specifically that you'd fired her. But if you knew she worked for Interpol, why help me?"

"The simplest answer is that you are my fated mate."

"I'm your what? Never mind. I'm not your anything. Give me a reason I can believe."

"I would caution you about listening to your tigress' instinctive reaction to snarl at me. When I haul you across my lap to slap your ass silly, it will not be she that feels my wrath. But the other reason is, I liked your sister. I dislike the fact that she was killed, and I suspect it was done so someone could implicate me."

Rhys nodded. "Ah, so this gallant rescue isn't about me at all, but rather about making sure her death doesn't touch you. Good to know. Since you have a plane, would you mind dropping me off in London? I should really call the police. Someone broke into and searched my place and I planned to call the police. That wasn't you, was it?"

"Of course not, and you know it. We are flying directly to Runestone."

"Rune... what?" She shook her head and waved him off. "Doesn't matter. I'll just fly home on an airline jet. Do British Airways or Virgin fly from Sweden to England?"

"Runestone is your home now," he growled.

"No. My life and my home are in London, and they don't include you and all of this spy shit that got Maeve killed."

The SUV turned down the drive of a private airport, driving out onto the tarmac and pulling to a stop in front of a private jet. Lars got out and after she ignored his extended hand, he reached into the backseat and extracted her.

"I don't want to go with you," she said, trying to push him away.

"That is of no matter. You will either accompany me onto the plane or I will carry you."

"I'll scream."

"Go ahead. There is no one here that is not in my employ. Consent may be important in a BDSM club like Baker Street, but here in the real world it is often simply ignored, especially when the one screaming is a misbehaving mate. We are going home, Rhys. You can either behave yourself or…"

She managed to jerk her arm away. "Or what?

You'll bite me? That was you, right? You did bite me while we were having sex?"

Rhys wasn't sure why she'd expected his men to be shocked, but they weren't. In fact, they all looked rather bored as they scanned the surrounding area, but for what?

"I claimed you, as the males of our kind have always claimed their mates."

"'Our kind?' I have news for you, you and I couldn't be more different. And your mate? Did you just call me your mate?" she said, annoyed that he didn't seem all that concerned that she was pissed that he'd bitten her.

"I did. Come along, mate, I want us airborne as quickly as possible. By telling the police Maeve worked for Interpol, you have given them a leg up. Depending on Interpol's end game, a collaboration between the two could become a problem. Come along, Rhys."

"I'm not going anywhere with you."

Shaking his head, he used his hold on her wrist to pull her forward while bending and putting his shoulder into her lower body. The next thing she knew, she was upside down, shouting and beating ineffectively at his back as he carried her up the steps into the plane. Rhys pummeled him until his large hand landed a stinging swat to her upturned rump.

"Enough," he growled.

His men followed them up the stairs and took

their seats as he eased her down into the seat by the window, blocking her exit with his imposing body.

"Doesn't it bother you that I don't want to go with you, and I think you capable of killing my sister?"

Lars sat down beside her buckling her seatbelt and speaking only as the plane's jet engines came to life and they began to taxi down the runway. A sort of lethargy seemed to be settling over her like a shroud.

"Not especially. You knew who I was when you came to my bed in Baker Street, so you thought you knew what I was capable of. As for your reticence to take your place at my side," he said, shrugging his massive shoulders, "it doesn't bother me at all. The best tigresses are often not brought easily to heel."

The plane gathered speed and lifted off easily, banking north and flying toward a destination she knew nothing about, but which seemed to be beckoning her home. As her tigress had receded to the furthest corner of her mind, Rhys allowed herself to relax as she gazed out the window, eventually closing her eyes to sleep.

CHAPTER 12

The purring seemed to have settled her. Lars could sense her tigress no longer prowled through the corridors of her mind. Perhaps it just recognized that the place to provoke a confrontation was not at more than forty thousand feet above the earth.

It had taken all his willpower to keep from storming into the morgue and tearing that cop limb from limb. How dare they take Rhys into the morgue, the actual morgue, not the viewing room, and force her to identify her sister? The tag on the drawer indicated they knew who she was. It had been unnecessary and cruel. It had also been designed to trip her up and put her off her game to see if they could get her to admit something or at least tell them something they didn't know. Lars snorted. That wouldn't take much.

He watched her sleep. She was, in his opinion, extraordinarily beautiful and his cock reminded him it wanted back inside her sooner rather than later. But that would have to wait until they were back in Runestone.

His mobile phone buzzed. Looking at the caller ID, he answered. "Björn? We're in the sky. We should be home…" he checked his watch, "in about five hours. Is there a problem?"

"There might be. You've been out of touch."

"I know Maeve is dead and they've found the body, but the French police being the French police, think the killer might be Rhys."

"Not just the French police…"

"What do you mean, not just the French police?" asked Lars, pushing the weariness worrying about her had caused to the side.

"Scotland Yard and Interpol have got it into their heads that your mate has stolen a valuable painting from Lloyds, leaving a fake behind."

"What the hell would make them think that?"

"The fact that Lloyd's has verified the painting she was set to authenticate is in fact a forgery. When Scotland Yard went to arrest her, they found she'd cleared out…"

"I'd planned to do that, to bring some of her things to Runestone to make her feel more at home, but I was clear…"

"It wasn't us, Lars. The man you left watching the

place has no idea how it happened. When he was having the window she went through replaced, he checked her flat thoroughly to see if he could tell if the two goons who went after her had taken anything."

"And did they?" growled Lars, ameliorating his tone and his emotions as he saw the effect his growing anger was having on Rhys' sleep. He had to remember that the bonding link seemed to have snapped on in full force.

"Not that we can tell. They had nothing with them when they left the apartment, but Oskar is convinced they or someone came back. Her laptop is missing, and whoever took it used her carry bag and took the charger. They also took her purse with her ID, cash, and credit cards. Some of her clothes appear to be missing, as well as her mobile phone."

"In other words, someone staged her flat to look as though she's stolen the painting and is on the lam."

"Precisely. Lloyd's has reported to Scotland Yard that a valuable, previously unknown painting by Raphael is missing, as is the woman who was verifying its authenticity. The 'forgery' has been discovered in the missing painting's place. They've put out the word they're looking for her and she is believed to have left England. Interpol has issued a red notice."

"She will need new identification and credit cards as well as a passport…"

"Under her name?"

"Rhys Jakobsson. Show her as a Swedish citizen with a Swedish passport. She's sleeping…"

"No, I'm awake. What's happened?" asked Rhys, rubbing the sleep from her eyes.

Lars held up one finger and spoke into the phone. "I want it ready when we land, and I'll have the plane go below radar and come in from the backside. Have the hangar open with the other jet, the prop plane and both helicopters inside. Any drones are to be shot down. Let our people know what's happening. We'll see you as soon as we can. I'll want a full report of everything we know as soon as we're secure at Runestone."

Lars ended the call and looked back at Rhys. "Are you hungry?"

"I want to know why you called me Rhys Jakobsson and seem to be getting me a phony passport."

"Answer my question, Rhys, are you hungry?"

"Not particularly and I don't usually eat with people who kidnap me."

"Interesting. Have you been kidnapped often?" he asked, allowing the corners of his mouth to lift in a seductive smile.

"You're not nearly as charming or as funny as you think you are," she snapped, rubbing her temples, closing her eyes and willing the headache that was starting to go away.

Not just the headache but this whole nightmare that had started when Maeve went missing. The icy fingers of remembrance wrapped around her heart and squeezed. Maeve wasn't just missing. She was dead. Rhys had identified her cold, lifeless body for the police in Lyon.

The soft purring began again.

"Knock it off. I am not a small child to be lulled out of a bad temper or my grief. My sister is dead, and I am not entirely convinced that you aren't responsible. In fact, even if you didn't kill her or order it done, I still place part of the responsibility on you."

Nodding, Lars said, "I can see where you would feel that way and won't even deny that your sister's investigation into my organization may have contributed to her death, but in that case, you have to admit that Interpol also shares in the responsibility."

"Oh, I haven't even begun with those bastards."

"I wouldn't disagree with your assessment. Quit evading my question. As to the purring, I will try to curb my need to offer you solace. I know you must be upset and only sought to make things easier for you."

Rhys leaned forward, invading his personal space. Lars did not move at all. "Answer my question."

"I am having new identification made for you as your British ones under Rhys Donovan have been flagged by both Scotland Yard and Interpol."

"What for? I haven't done anything illegal. Well, I did punch that Interpol guy…"

Lars chuckled. "So, you have always possessed the spirit of a tigress. The Gift merely set her free."

"What gift? And what's the Red Notice for?"

"The Gift is what allowed your tigress to come forward. I'm surprised she made herself known so forcefully so quickly."

"How did I acquire this 'Gift?'"

"It was initiated when I grasped your neck in my claiming bite."

"'Grasped?' You didn't grasp my neck, you asshole, you bit me."

"I believe I said that. It is called a claiming *bite* for a reason."

"So that's why I can…" She seemed to be searching for a word.

"Shift is the term you are looking for. You can shift from your human self to that of a white tigress and back again at will. I suspect you already know that your human part is the one in control unless your tigress feels threatened. Tell me about the men who broke into your flat."

"Not so fast," Rhys said, shaking her head. "I'm not through with my questions yet. Why has Interpol issued a Red Notice on me?"

"They believe you have stolen a painting."

"A painting? What painting? Who would tell them that?"

"I don't have all the details, but it seems someone at Lloyd's has reported the theft of a Raphael and that they believe you took it and put a forgery in its place. Your flat has been staged to make it appear as though you have taken off with it."

"That's ridiculous," she stated. "I was asked to verify a previously unknown Raphael, but my report... Shit! I had it saved in my draft folder on my computer. I was feeling like crap—is that from your little love nip?"

"One of the things they took was your computer so whatever you wrote and to whom has no knowledge of that."

Rhys flopped back against her seat, and asked, fearing she knew the answer, "Is the forgery still there?"

"I'm afraid so, and it's been labeled as such. The working theory was you exchanged the original for the fake and were going to verify the fake as genuine."

Rubbing her forehead with her fingers, she said, "Someone set me up. The Raphael was a forgery. It could pass a cursory inspection but there were so many things off about it." She sighed. "I am so screwed."

"Not yet, but I will take care of that when we get home."

Rhys glared at him. "Again, not funny."

"Not meant to be. I intend to take you to my bed and keep you there for a while. You will be safe at Runestone. No one saw you board the plane or even saw us take off. We are flying in from the off side of the island and will land and pull the plane into the hangar before we disembark."

"If someone's watching, they'll see us leave the hangar."

He shook his head. "No, they won't. The hangar doors will close, and we will access Runestone via the underground tunnel. Besides, it is very difficult for them to know what happens on the estate. Our security is vital to keeping our secret. The estate itself is walled and we have both electronic surveillance as well as security patrols. We routinely set off EMPs around our perimeter. You will be safe."

"EMP?"

"Electro Magnetic Pulse. It can be aimed so that it totally knocks out anything that has an electrical charge, even if it's only from a battery."

"What will you do if they come knocking with a warrant for my arrest?"

"I will keep you safe." He took her hand in his, rubbing his thumb across the back of it and glad that she didn't snatch it back. "I will never allow them to take you from me. A Red Notice is not a warrant for your arrest, it is a request to detain you. It's just a way for Interpol to get help trying to find someone or keep them on a no-fly list. The police could take you in for questioning if they had a reasonable suspicion that you were guilty of something and that you were at Runestone, but with no one even seeing you in

Gotland, they would be hard pressed to make that claim."

That seemed to appease her.

"I have to find out who killed my sister and who is responsible for setting me up," she said quietly.

"We will see it done. I suspect the two are interrelated and we cannot solve one mystery without solving the other. I will become a regular *Wallander*."

"Didn't he work alone?"

"Yes, but he was a brilliant detective and never failed to solve a case."

"The alone part won't work for me."

"You will remain where I can keep you safe," he growled low.

"You don't know much about me, do you? I may not have worked for Interpol, but my sister wasn't the only one with a reputation for being bull dogged about finding things out. You either include me, or I'll do it on my own."

"You will not, but why give me a choice?" he asked suspiciously.

Rhys gestured to the plane. "You have money and connections, but I'm the one who knows the art world, knows a forgery when I see it, and knows a lot of the major players. For instance, I know you don't steal art, but you broker deals for those who do. Besides, as you have already noted, at this moment, I'm a woman without a country and you can supply me with the documentation I need. I am not unmindful that they murdered my sister, who was a trained and skilled field agent."

"No."

"You don't get to tell me no, asshole."

"You will not speak to me that way. The next time will cost you five hard over my knee."

"You have no idea what a pain in the ass I can be," she retorted.

"I'm beginning to understand. What you don't understand is that while you are figuratively a pain in my ass, I will be a literal one on yours. I understand and appreciate your devotion to your sister. If I were to agree to give you some limited form of participation in finding your sister's killer and who framed you, how would you see this playing out?"

"I was thinking a kind of Nick and Nora Charles."

He nodded slowly. "Who?"

"They were in a series of movies and were a high society couple who solved mysteries together, with Nora often getting herself in trouble along the way."

"No. I may be willing to include you in knowing what we are doing, I will not allow you to be put in danger. You will not leave Runestone without my permission. Agreed?"

She smiled slowly as she nodded her head; Lars didn't believe her for a moment. Rhys turned back to the window. He wanted to respect her wishes not to be soothed, but it was difficult. He wanted more than anything to take her in his arms and lull her back to sleep. He could feel her fear, confusion, and grief rolling down the tether to him and wondered when it had happened that one little human had come to mean the world to him. He vowed to himself to make this right for her, whatever it took.

CHAPTER 13

Maeve was dead. She would never hear her sister's laughter again. There would be no more making a meal together, getting a couple of beers or a glass of wine and binge watching what were commonly known as 'chick flicks.' No more unexpected phone calls when one of them was feeling down just because the other could sense it, even from far away. She'd heard of twins being that close, but Maeve was, no, had been, four years older.

If Lars was to be believed, and Rhys' instincts told her she could trust what he said, even if she didn't trust the man himself—he'd had nothing to do with her sister's death. She could easily believe he hadn't killed her himself or ordered it done, but she was convinced Maeve's assignment to try and infiltrate and bring down his criminal organization was a proximate cause of her death. But if Lars bore a minor part of the responsibility, Interpol bore the majority.

Rhys didn't want to close her eyes. Every time she did, she saw Maeve—not the smiling and laughing sister who had always greeted her, but her sister's cold, dead corpse when the morgue attendant had pulled back the sheet covering her body. It had taken everything in Rhys not to throw up. The pain and grief had overwhelmed her, but somehow, she had known she had to keep her wits about her, and puking all over everything wasn't consistent with that need.

How had Maeve been killed? From what she'd been able to observe, there'd been no obvious bullet or stab wounds. No evidence of garroting. So that left, as the most likely causes, strangulation or poison. She wondered if she was entitled to a copy of the autopsy report. She knew they would give her, as next of kin, a copy of the death certificate, which should list cause of death, but she wanted a copy of the report. In order to find her sister's killer, she would need to know that.

Rhys had been running on adrenaline ever since this whole nightmare had begun. She'd had the brief respite when she'd slept in the warehouse, but it hadn't been a deep, restorative sleep. Instead, she'd slept lightly and only then because she felt as though her tigress was keeping watch. It was a funny feeling, knowing she now shared a body with another entity. Oddly, it didn't frighten her or make her feel violated.

It was almost as if the universe had known Maeve was gone and given her the tigress so that she wouldn't be alone.

She shivered as tears began to slide down her cheeks. Resting her head against the plane's window, Rhys could feel Lars' deep rumbling wrapping around her as if it were one of Baker Street's cashmere blankets. She wanted to growl and make him stop, but right now she would admit, if only to herself, that she was in need of comforting.

What the hell had happened? Maeve was dead, lying in a morgue, murdered. Rhys was accused of the theft of a major work of art. For the time being she was stuck with a gangster as her protector, and she was no longer human. That last little bit might not turn out to be so bad. After all, it had been her tigress that had saved her.

Bringing her hands up to her face, she wiped her tears away and sat back. "So, tell me about this whole shifter thing."

"We have existed alongside humans and purebreds for longer than anyone can remember. We are stronger, faster, and live a healthier, longer life. All in all, we are the superior species. We live amongst the humans, hidden in plain sight."

"If you're…"

"We're," he corrected.

Inclining her head, she nodded. "If *we're* so superior, why hide?"

"Because we do not wish to be at war with humans or tigers. So, we live parallel lives, moving amongst humans without their knowledge of our existence."

"Your Berserker Syndicate, are they all…?"

"White tigers? Yes. My clan has held Runestone since the time of the Vikings."

"So, some of the Vikings were like you?"

Lars smiled, indulgently. "Like us, but yes. Our ability to shift has allowed us to live and thrive in environments not hospitable to humans. In the beginning, there were fewer of us. And then, as now, males outnumbered females."

Rhys straightened up. "So, your males 'gifted' this on unsuspecting human females."

"There was a time when we eschewed those who were not born with the Gift. We chose instead to share a mate—two or three different males to a single female. Male tigers being what we are, that led to a lot of bloodshed and unnecessary violence and didn't alter the fact that we needed more females…"

"I don't imagine the females were overly enamored with the idea either."

"Not necessarily. We found as we evolved that the males of our kind could initiate the Gift by claiming a human female…"

"Biting her…" she supplied with an arched eyebrow, daring him to challenge her assertion.

Lars didn't rise to the bait. "The claiming bite

initiates an override of human DNA, overlaying it with our own."

"So how do tigresses turn a human male?"

"Only men can bestow the Gift."

"Why does that not surprise me?" she asked sarcastically.

"As you will see, and probably have surmised, ours is a male-dominated society."

"Of course, it is. Let me ask you this—what happens if a tigress doesn't want to be mated?"

"Tigresses are expected to mate and produce offspring. Without them, our kind would die. It is why we cherish them and keep them safe."

"Lock them up and keep them as your plaything until you knock them up…"

"That is enough, *Skönhet*. For the most part our tigresses live long, happy lives. It's not like if their mate is killed, they are forced into another pairing… at least not any longer. As with humans, there was a time tigresses were used as political or dynastic pawns."

"I can see the big difference. Now you just turn unsuspecting women against their wills without bothering to tell them you did it." The accusation was clear in her tone.

Lars inhaled deeply, trying to rein in his temper. "You are my fated mate. Tigers are born knowing the scent of their fated mates and will act accordingly when they are near. Besides, had you stayed at my side where you belonged, I would have explained everything."

"You're really not getting the issue here, are you? You should have told me to begin with. Better yet, how about you ask me first?"

"What would you have said if I had asked you?"

"I'd have turned down your charming request."

Lars shrugged, seemingly unconcerned. "Thus, why I didn't ask."

"You're impossible," Rhys said, shrugging her shoulders.

"I am your alpha and your mate."

"I want a divorce."

"We are not yet formally bonded or married, but it changes nothing. You are my fated mate and mistress to our clan. You will act accordingly."

Rhys started to laugh. The enormity and severity of what had been done to her and what was happening made the sound border on hysteria. "If you believe that, it only shows you haven't been paying attention and don't know me at all."

"I know you are my fated mate," he said stubbornly. "You will act in accordance with your rank and responsibility."

"How's your clan going to feel about you hauling some human female home and installing her in your bed and in their lives?"

"There are some who may not like the idea at first, but they will accept and respect you. I won't lie to you and tell you that there aren't those who are prejudiced against those who are turned. They believe those not born a shifter are inferior and they would call you 'half-blood.' It is not a distinction that is allowed in our clan. Should anyone treat you with anything less than the respect you deserve, you are to tell me, and I will deal with them."

"That ought to make me real popular. Thanks, Lars, but I can fight my own battles." She shook her head in disbelief, unable to truly accept any of it, including Maeve's death. "You don't get it, do you? Putting the whole tiger-shifter thing aside, what makes you think I would willingly get involved with you?"

"You were willing enough at Baker Street," he growled.

"To do a scene with you? To play with you? To fuck you? Sure. But I have no interest in being the mistress of a gangster. Maeve may have been the one to work for Interpol, but there is nothing about you or those who run criminal organizations that hold any allure for me. Your arrogance and disregard for the law aside, we come back round to the whole you stole my fucking humanity."

"Watch your language, and I stole nothing from you." The gentle tone and rumble coming down the link was gone and quickly being replaced with irritation. "I gifted you with a longer, healthier life. You should be grateful."

"Hot news flash. I'm not. In case you missed it, I'm pretty pissed about it."

"What would you have me do? Reverse it? And before you say yes, know that it cannot be done. Should I banish you from the clan and leave you to fend for yourself? Let you go after whoever killed Maeve? Let them kill you? This, *Skönhet*, I will not do."

"Quit calling me that. I am not a beauty."

"Enough. No one will speak about my mate in a derogatory way, including my mate."

"So, what is this mind meld thing we have going? Do I have that with everyone?"

Lars took a deep breath, trying to regain control of his rising temper. "No. It only exists between bonded mates. I can understand what an ordeal this has been."

"Ordeal?" she snorted. "My sister is dead. She was my only family…"

He leaned over taking her hands in his. Rhys tried to pull away, but Lars held tight. "You are no longer alone. You have me."

"Only until somebody kills you. And what makes you think I want you?"

"You wanted me at Baker Street."

"It's a kink club where people have sex. Of course, I wanted you to get me off. That's part of why I went there."

"And the other part?"

"I thought I could get you to tell me what you knew about Maeve being missing."

He laughed. "You were playing out of your league, Rhys."

"Maybe, but so are you. Things aren't quite going the way you planned, are they?"

"Is that what frightens you, *Skönhet?* That I might be killed?" Rhys said nothing and refused to meet his eyes. Lars took her chin between his thumb and forefinger and lifted her head. "You will find in general that tigers are hard to kill, and I am harder to kill than most. But even if I were to fall, you are part of our clan and will always be treated with respect."

Rhys continued to try and pull away. "I don't want the life you are offering me."

"It is not an offer you can refuse," he said with a chuckle.

"Not even close to funny," she said, finally freeing herself.

"Nevertheless, it is the truth. You need a man who can match your spirit. I am that man and I have claimed you as my own. It will be fine, Rhys. We will find your sister's killers and make them pay, and we will clear your name."

Rhys turned back to the window. He made it sound so simple, and she supposed for Lars, it was. But it was not so simple for her. He was a gangster. He had stolen the very essence of who she was. If she wasn't human, then could she really be the sister Maeve had left behind?

The tigress within her prowled at the edges of her mind—hissing, her tail slowly wagging back and forth in agitation. *Easy girl. I'll never admit it to him, but I'm kind of glad you're here with me.* And that was the truth. If it hadn't been for the tigress, she most likely would be dead.

She closed her eyes and leaned her head against the window, feeling the resonant purring coming from Lars.

Lars. Now there was a conundrum. There was no denying she was wildly attracted to him, and her response to him at Baker Street had been off the charts. He called to something deep and dark inside her in a way no other man ever had. She'd even found she wanted to submit. He offered peace, but at what price? She'd never been one to sit around being pretty and doing nothing.

But what would she do now? Even if they cleared her name. No, wait, *when* they cleared her name, the taint of having been accused would never leave her. And her life was in London. Somehow, she doubted the leader of the Berserker Syndicate was going to allow his mate to live there.

A week ago, she thought her life settled and on some kind of steady trajectory. What the hell had happened? How was she going to get it back on track? The most disconcerting question remained—did she really want to? Regardless of what she told Lars, the attraction and compulsion to be with him tugged at her constantly.

If she could make him leave… if she could somehow find a way back to something resembling her former life… would she still want it? Or would this experience leave her fundamentally and irrevocably changed?

CHAPTER 14

*L*ars watched her sleep. She was exhausted—mentally, emotionally, and physically. Everything she'd been through since she left Baker Street had to have been an ordeal. Perhaps he should have spent time courting her and easing her into a relationship, but London was not Runestone, and his people and business needed him. Maeve—was there anything he could have done to save her, or to spare Rhys from the trauma that poxy French copper had put her through?

Quietly, he left his seat to retrieve a small pillow and soft, warm blanket. Slipping the pillow under her head and laying the blanket around her, he moved quietly, purring all the while, to allow her to sleep. Her tigress growled down the link. Lars shook his head. He'd never heard of the animal side of a shifter having such a presence and personality. But it was obvious the tigress was protective of Rhys and for that he thanked her, which seemed to pacify her ire if only a little bit.

"Alpha," said Leif. "There is food and drink. You need to take care of yourself if only so that you can care for your mate."

"I have no wish to be away from her, even if only for a few minutes."

Leif nodded. "I understand. I feel the same every time I leave Runestone."

Lars shook his head. "I didn't understand."

"I never said anything. It is my honor to travel with you."

"Even if you had, I wouldn't have understood. I always believed that fated mates were a fairytale we told the tigresses to justify forcing them into a pair bond they might not initially want."

"But now you know differently," Leif said with a grin. "I'll bring you something."

"Thank you. Bring me enough that if she wakes, I can share with her. I think right now she needs sleep more than anything." Leif stopped as if he had a question to ask. "Yes?"

Turning to look back at him, Leif asked, "Were you surprised she was able to shift so quickly?"

Lars nodded. "A bit, and even more that Rhys has been able to grasp and accept that she is no longer human. But then, I've never encountered a tigress with a spirit quite like the one that shares my mate's soul. Both of them are extraordinary."

Leif left him and was soon back with food and drink. Thanking him, Lars vowed to find a way to keep those of his men who were mated closer to home. He'd had her less than a day when he lost track of her, and it had been the worst day of his life. He vowed that in the future, he would always know where she was. He recognized now the sacrifice the men who left Runestone without their mates made for him. He knew now they had to be worried for their own mates, and most likely their mates had been worried for them. His job was to provide for all in his care. In the future, he would do a better job where his people and his mate were concerned.

Rhys stirred and he reached out to stroke her hair. Perhaps she would be less resistant to more tangible and tactile forms of comforting. She batted his hand away as if he was nothing more threatening than a bug. That alone, he supposed, was progress.

Pulling his laptop out, he began scanning news stories coming out of London about the art theft. Rhys was convinced that the theft of the Raphael and her sister's death were connected. If she was right, and he suspected she was, he wondered how those responsible would spin Maeve's murder. Would they try to pin that on Rhys, as well?

The two most obvious scenarios for them to use were that Maeve had tried to apprehend Rhys or that the two had been in it together and Rhys had turned on her sister. It was hard for him to believe anyone would believe either tale. He hadn't known Maeve long or well, but he had known the bond to her sister had been strong. He brooded as he thought about their last exchange, thought about what, if anything, he might have done differently.

"We know you're working for Interpol, Mara," Lars said, angrily, wondering if Interpol had sent her or if she had gone to them.

"I don't know what you're talking about," she answered, trying to sound innocent and a bit frightened by her intimidating boss.

"Don't lie to me. You were the only one outside those who were there who knew about the meeting, and it was only by sheer luck and cunning that we were able to escape the noose you tried to slip around our necks."

"Mr. Jakobsson, I don't know what you're talking about. I knew that you had a business meeting, some kind of deal you were brokering, but that's all I knew."

Lars shook his head. "No, it isn't. My cybersecurity people found where you hacked in to get the information you needed to pass on to Interpol."

Mara's shoulders slumped. As an operative there was a point you knew your cover was irretrievably blown and survival became your only goal.

"What now?" she asked quietly, as if resigned to whatever fate he assigned her.

"You're fired. You'll be escorted from the premises. Get out

of Sweden. Don't ever let me catch you near me or my organization again."

She nodded. *"For what it's worth? I have never been able to figure you out. I have had to continually remind myself that you're a gangster, but I can't help but feel that you're actually one of the good guys. My final report will be to tell Interpol I think there are better and bigger fish to fry than you."*

"What will you do?" he asked, conversationally.

"I had planned to take a long weekend with my sister in Vienna. We want to go to the Spanish Riding School."

"You have a sister?"

"I do, and if you ever try to hurt her, I'll make sure Interpol never has to worry about you again," she answered, fiercely.

"I wish you well, Mara, but take care, as others do not."

"Are you threatening me?"

Lars shook his head. "Not at all. You have caused me a minor inconvenience. You know me well enough to know that it would take more than that for me to retaliate. But if we figured it out, others may have done so, as well. They might not be as forgiving."

Maeve started for the door, but then turned back, as if undecided. "If I walked away from Interpol and asked for your protection for my sister and myself?"

"I would give it, but it would have to be both of you. Otherwise, your sister could be used against you or us. You should have a care where your sister is concerned."

"I will, and I'll talk to her in Vienna. I'm tired, Lars. Maybe it's time to come in from the cold."

"You and your sister will always be welcome at Runestone's hearth."

She'd nodded and then turned on her heel and had been escorted out of the building, and he'd thought out of his life. He'd been wrong.

Rhys woke with a start. "Where am I?"

"You're still on the plane, Rhys. We have another hour or so until we set down at Runestone. There's food and drink if you'd like something."

"Maeve's dead, isn't she? I mean, I didn't just dream that."

"No, *Skönhet*. Your sister was murdered."

"And I'm being framed for stealing a Raphael that was a forgery," she said, looking at him for confirmation.

How he wished he could dispel her fears and concerns. "That, too, is correct. Although they have yet to issue a warrant for your arrest."

"The two are connected, aren't they?"

"That would be my guess. Maeve was trying to bring down my organization through our smuggling and brokering of deals of certain items with a less than bulletproof provenance."

That made her smile. "That's a really nice way to say it."

"I thought so," he said with a grin.

"I think the two are connected."

He wanted her to lead the discussion. "As do I. It seems too coincidental that Maeve and Interpol were coming after me for art theft or at least the brokering of it and Maeve's sister—that would be you—is being sought for questioning in connection with a stolen Raphael."

"That's not all. What's happened? If you want me to trust you, you need to be honest with me."

Lars nodded. "Nothing else has happened—at least nothing I can find on regular and social media, but I have our cyber people monitoring both situations. I suspect at some point they'll try and link you to Maeve's death."

Rhys slumped back in her seat. "They think I killed Maeve."

"I don't know that anyone really believes that, but I do think they will try to lay that at your doorstep as well."

Leaning forward, she grasped his beer bottle, took a sip and returned it to his hand, and then reached for some of the cheese. "Sorry. I nibble when I'm thinking or worrying."

"Good to know. What's mine is yours and you never need to apologize or ask."

She laughed ruefully. "Careful Jakobsson. You have a lot of money and if I have to go on the lam, I could clean you out."

"I meant what I said. I already have new credit cards, bank account and identification, including a passport, being prepared."

"Just like that?" she asked, snapping her fingers.

"Not exactly. I never said I would set you free to run amok on your own. I told you we are mates, and I will provide and care for you. Whoever is doing this will be made to pay one way or another. They will be held to account and judgment will be given."

"I suppose I should say that I want them arrested and put away forever. And I do, but if that can't happen, I want them to pay—not for what they've done to me, but for killing my sister."

"You two were close."

"We were. I was thinking earlier that even though we were born four years apart, we often had that twin thing going where we know if the other one is in trouble. But not always." Sadness touched her eyes.

"You didn't know about her death, did you?"

Rhys shook her head. "No. The last time we spoke, we were planning to meet in Vienna."

"To see the white stallions at the Spanish Riding School?"

"Yes, how did you know that?"

"I liked your sister, and she was very good at her job. When I fired her, I asked what her plans were. She told me she was meeting her sister in Vienna." He smiled remembering Maeve's ferocity, a trait she shared with her younger sister.

"She told you that?" Rhys asked.

"Yes. Right before she threatened to kill me if I ever harmed you."

Rhys' eyes grew warm. "She could be like that. Did you know we both rode as kids?"

"No. Remember, I didn't know much about her real life at all."

"Oh, right," Rhys said, a bit embarrassed. "Well, we did. We both rode dressage. Maeve stuck with it."

"And you?"

"I did three-day eventing—dressage, cross country, and show jumping."

"Why did you give it up?"

"When our parents were killed by a drunk driver, we were sent to live with our mother's brother and his family. They didn't have money for things like that, but still managed to burn through our inheritance. Luckily, our parents had been able to specifically earmark the money for our education. Maeve left when she was eighteen. I was able to get an emancipated minor status and get out when I was sixteen, but the damage was done. We both had money for college, but not much else."

"I'm sorry."

A light lit up her eyes as if a happy memory had been brought up. "We never were. We used to laugh about the fact that we probably would have been the worst trust fund kids that ever lived. Instead, we depended on each other and learned to work for what we wanted. Horses were just a luxury we couldn't afford."

"There are stables and horses at Runestone. Many

of our people ride. If there isn't a horse that suits you, we will find one that does."

"That's a lovely thought, Lars, but I'm not looking past finding my sister's killer and clearing my name."

"Have you ever considered working for yourself—offering your services as a freelance expert?"

"The space and equipment to set up to do restoration and verification of paintings and other *objects d'art* is an expensive undertaking." She arched her eyebrow at him. "I won't authenticate a forgery."

"I wouldn't ask you to, but your skills could be valuable to my business and money is not an object. Think about it. I cannot see you being content with being the pampered mistress of the clan. If it's something that appeals to you, we can set it up." He held up his hand to ward off her argument. "One step at a time, *Skönhet*. Let's catch your sister's killer and clear your name first. Perhaps you will see that I am right about your status as my fated mate."

"Don't get your hopes up," she warned.

"Even your tigress knows I'm your mate although she's a fierce thing. You two seem to have a far different connection than the rest of us."

"How so?"

"While we are all aware of our altered selves, I've never been sure if they are truly aware of us. It also seemed like the two of you communicated directly and she had no trouble reaching down the tether and communicating with me."

Rhys' eyebrows knitted together in confusion. "You, and others like you don't talk or communicate with your other selves?"

"No. We are aware, but mostly we simply call our tiger forward or demand they relinquish control. The two of you, from what I can tell, are far more aware—your tigress is far more sentient, and you are each aware of and concerned for the other."

"And you aren't?" Lars shook his head. "Then you're doing it wrong," she stated with certainty.

Lars chuckled and then began to indicate points of interest as they approached Runestone. He was beginning to think his mate might be right.

CHAPTER 15

Rhys realized she knew very little about Sweden. The only thing that came to mind when she even gave it a thought was the Muppets' character, the Swedish Chef. Another entire country she knew nothing about.

On more than one occasion, Maeve had suggested that at some point they just travel the world. The thought of her sister made her heart clench. So much they'd never done. They'd been robbed of so much time. The only solace she had, apart from what seemed like an instinctive response on Lars' part to try and comfort her, was that they had never left anything unsaid. Neither of them had ever allowed any disagreement to fester or go unresolved. And never had they parted, either in person or via electronic device, that they didn't tell each other 'I love you.'

"My curious mate," Lars mused softly.

"Apart from the obvious—I do not accept that I am your anything, much less your mate—how so?"

"I could feel your grief about your sister, but it passed almost as quickly as it came."

"I just remembered that even though she was taken from me, she passed without needing to say anything to me that I needed to hear or vice versa. I think because our parents were taken from us so dramatically and without warning, we never left things unresolved between us, nor ever failed to say, 'I love you.' It was kind of ingrained that life is short and unpredictable. So, while I am obviously sad that someone ended my sister's life, at least I don't have the 'if only we hadn't parted in anger, or I wish I'd told her…' At least we were spared that."

"I would think that is a lot more than most people have."

"Lars, you need to know I would never tell anyone about your people being shifters." She gave a nervous laugh. "For one thing, who would believe me? Oh, they might believe if I shifted in front of them, but then they'd know about me, too."

"It never occurred to me that you would betray us."

"I thought about asking you if it was something that could be undone, but you said it couldn't, and even if it could, I realized I'm not sure I'd want to. She is a part of me and especially with Maeve gone, I fear I would miss her presence. But," she said, arching her eyebrow at him, "you might have asked *before* you did it."

"And again, what would you have answered, assuming I could convince you I wasn't delusional?"

"Probably no."

"Thus, the reason I didn't ask. I know you refuse to accept that we are fated mates, although my guess is that your tigress has confirmed that fact, but I knew. Male tigers have been claiming unwilling tigresses for as long as we have existed."

"That doesn't make it right, and it doesn't mean she and I will ever accept it."

She turned away from him, hoping he couldn't feel the chaotic combination of emotions that swirled all around her. There was no denying, even if only to herself, that there was a part of her that knew what he said was true. It was almost as if she'd been waiting for him all her life. There was even a part of her that somehow knew he was right and that they belonged together, but she couldn't afford to forget that he was a gangster, that he had taken a part of her humanity, and that he might be far more involved in her sister's murder than he cared to admit. The latter was the thing she needed to keep uppermost in her mind until she knew the truth.

"When we arrive at Runestone, your things..."

"You do realize my things consist of a few toiletries, a change of clothes, some duplicate identification and that's about it," she interrupted him without turning around.

"I did in fact realize and so arranged to have things from some of the shops in Visby sent to the stronghold. If you don't like them, you can make a list and I will send someone to Stockholm."

She turned in her seat to look at him. "Am I to be a prisoner at Runestone?"

He took a deep breath, and Rhys could feel him fighting to remain calm. "You are mistress to our clan. Runestone is your home. I would remind you that Interpol has put a Red Notice on your passport and credit cards. They want you for questioning for both the theft of the Raphael..."

"The forged one. The painting I worked on was not authenticated."

Lars nodded. "While true, that is not how it is being portrayed. They want to question you both about the Raphael as well as your sister's death. And Scotland Yard has been making noise about the alleged theft. It would be inadvisable for you to be simply walking around Stockholm."

Much as she wanted to disagree with him, she knew he was right. "Any ideas how we might handle either or both of those?"

"Without your research and notes," he said, "it will be difficult to prove that the Raphael they have was the same one you had deemed to be a fake."

"But doesn't that mean that they can't prove there was ever another one there?"

"Unfortunately, no. The owner who sent it to be authenticated says they have provenance and that it was genuine. While your authentication cannot be bought, I assure you that others are not as honorable. He says he can prove it was genuine."

"What about Laura? I work with her at Lloyd's. I told her my suspicions."

"Did you put it in writing? Did she confirm them? Did she ever examine the picture?"

"Well, no."

"Precisely, so even if she was willing to back you up, she has nothing more than you telling her that. What do you know about her?"

"Laura?"

"Yes. I find it interesting that she has said nothing in your defense. She has been completely silent on the matter."

Rhys considered what he'd said. He was right about Stockholm. If she was taken in for questioning, she wouldn't be free to investigate her sister's murder or to prove her innocence with regard to the Raphael.

"That is odd about Laura," she agreed.

"Is there any chance she is part of whatever this is?"

"I wouldn't think so," said Rhys, slowly shaking her head. "We were friends, but not overly close. But I find it hard to believe she would either frame me or have anything to do with some kind of insurance fraud…" Her voice trailed off.

"What?" he asked.

"I can't believe Laura would have anything to do with fraud or a stolen painting…"

"But?" One of his eyebrows arched up.

"The painting came to us through her boyfriend, Anton Petrov. He has a gallery…"

"Which is most likely a front for laundering money and a host of other illegal activities."

"Why do you say that?" she asked, trying to sound outraged for her friend, but knowing that she'd most likely been right not to trust him.

"Anton is Uri Petrov's son. Petrov is head of one of the most powerful bratva families. We need to make sure Knight knows that Petrov's son is operating in London."

"Knight? Joshua Knight? You don't know that Anton is involved. Maybe he's made a break from his father."

Lars shook his head. "You don't make a break from the bratva and live to tell about it. You sure as hell don't do it and run a gallery in London."

"If Anton is his son…"

"He is Uri's son, and Uri wouldn't care. He'd kill Anton himself just to make the point. If your friend Laura is involved with Anton, we need to get her to safety."

"You just assume she has nothing to do with it?"

Lars nodded. "You're a good judge of character—your assessment of mine notwithstanding. If she's your friend, she's a good person."

"Do you think that's what's at the heart of it—insurance fraud?" she asked, biting her lower lip.

"Could very well be. Or it could be that they planned to try and pass off a forgery and blame it on me. Right now, the bratva would like to be able to bring those organizations straddling the fence on their side. Discrediting me would help. Besides, it's the only thing that makes any kind of sense. Otherwise, why try and pass off a forgery?"

"But how does it tie to my sister?"

"Interpol managed to get her embedded in my organization and she was behind this deal. If it went through and I got blamed for the fraud, it's bad. If it gets out that I've been infiltrated by Interpol, it's bad. Either way, the fallout rains down on my head." Lars pursed his lips and then allowed a small smile to form. "It's kind of ingenious if you think about it."

"There is no way my sister is involved in any kind of insurance fraud."

"Not knowingly, no." He chuckled. "If your sister was corruptible in any way, I would have found out about it and exploited it for my own use—turned her back against Interpol as it were. But she wasn't, thus why I called her out, fired her, and sent her home. But what if her death had nothing to do with me and my organization and everything to do with the Raphael?"

"I don't see how that could be."

"Did you ever mention to her your suspicions about the Raphael?"

Rhys started to deny it but stopped. "I don't know how it fits, but one of the reasons I could get away to meet her in Vienna was because I knew I would be able to write my report regarding my authenticity verification. Do you think…"

"What?"

"Did you or do you have any brokering deals where the painting in question is a Raphael?"

"Not that I am aware of, but then I don't know every single deal we have brewing. The part of my business that deals with art is just one of my divisions and not even a particularly big one, although it is fairly lucrative."

"They didn't get Al Capone through his racketeering and murder, they nailed him for taxes. Maeve once said, it's often the smaller areas of a syndicate that are the most vulnerable. Do you do any kind of verification?"

"No, but it wouldn't be unheard of for someone to want to hold me responsible if a fraud had been perpetrated. Some of the deals, in fact a great many of them, have parties that are, shall we say, less than on the up and up."

"Could it be used to discredit you?"

"Perhaps or perhaps to disrupt the art trade

through Sweden. Officially, Sweden was neutral during World War II."

"That was a long time ago."

Lars nodded, "But Europe, Scandinavia, and the UK have long memories. For some the scars of that war and all its fallout still resonate, and there are syndicates in Germany and Russia that could see my demise and that of my organization as advantageous."

"Do you really think that's what's going on?"

"Hard to say. It's one possibility. It could be that the bratva see Gotland Island as a unique opportunity to be the ruling power."

"So, you don't get along with the bratva?"

He laughed. "Sweetheart, even the bratva don't get along with the bratva. They are brutal men who are loyal only to themselves. So, if you're one of the various families that make up the bratva you could raise your standing considerably if you controlled Gotland Island. We will figure it out and those responsible for your sister's death will be made to face judgment for it."

"I need to think about something else. Tell me about Runestone. Maeve said it was a monastery at one point?"

"Yah. It started out as a monastic estate and then became a fortress because of its strategic position on the island and its proximity to Visby. It is one of two fortresses, with Visborg Castle being within the town itself. Runestone is older and holds a better view of incoming danger. It is not what many think of as a castle with rounded turrets and the like. It looks far more like the great estates in Britain that are thought of as manor houses. It does have an interior bailey and it also has a true moat that surrounds it. We can see and smell the sea as the entire island is less than 1,230 square miles but we don't sit on a cliff where you can hear the sea crashing below like Sabu in Norway or Hammerfall in Denmark."

"I would think, as it was once a monastery, that it is fairly remote?"

"Yes, very, but difficult to conquer. We do sit upon a promontory hill with great open fields and grounds surrounding us, then a vast moat, and then more open land until you get to the forest that surrounds the entire area."

"So, almost like an island within an island."

"Exactly. I often marvel at the engineering that must have gone on, not only in its creation, but in that of the setting and the escape routes. There are reinforced escape routes that go on for miles."

"Like the one from the hangar to the castle itself?"

"Exactly. The hangar is difficult to see, and it is not easy to access our landing strip. So, once we land and secure the hangar, which I had built to withstand having a bomb dropped on it, we are completely secure."

"How do I get across the moat?"

"You don't. I do not want you outside Runestone's walls—at least not until I, or we, know what is going on."

"What if I don't want to stay—now or later?"

"The choice is not yours. You are my mate, and it is best that you begin to settle yourself with that idea. We use small boats to get across the moat. It would be difficult to swim its width."

She looked at him, lifting her chin ever so slightly. "Tigresses are excellent swimmers."

"Yes, they are. But then, so are their mates."

"My apologies for interrupting, Alpha, but we are about to make the final approach. The pilot wanted me to remind both of you to buckle up."

Rhys turned back towards the window and gasped in awe at her first sight of Runestone. Her mate—no, not her mate. She wasn't sure exactly what he was, but he wasn't her mate—had sold it short. It was enormous and breathtakingly beautiful.

'Never fear,' purred her tigress, *'I can swim that moat.'* And Rhys had no doubt she could.

CHAPTER 16

As the plane banked and made its approach to the landing strip, Rhys could see why Lars had said it was tricky. As far as she could tell, it wasn't overly long and seemed to dead end into a hangar tucked under the trees. She had to agree with Lars' assessment that it would be difficult for anyone to spot her once the plane pulled into the hangar.

As he set down gently on the runway, Rhys had to admit the pilot was good at his job. They rolled into the hangar, and not once had she felt like he was standing on the brakes to get the plane stopped. As soon as they were inside, Rhys could hear the mechanized doors closing to keep prying eyes, and people, out. The plane powered down and the stairway was lowered. Lars offered her his hand and taking it, she deplaned.

Even the hangar was enormous, clean and well-organized. There was a second plane as well as two helicopters—one much larger than the other—parked inside. There also looked to be a large service/workshop area, various hydraulic lifts, chains, and a nicely appointed food and loading area.

"This is impressive," said Rhys.

"Thank you. It allows us to do business without someone easily monitoring our comings and goings. The stairwell to the left goes down and leads back to the castle. The one to the right leads to a sort of staging area with golf carts and the tunnel that leads to a building on the edge of the estate that functions as our garage. There are a number of cars there, as well as a driveway to a gate entrance."

"You do value your privacy."

Lars nodded. "As have all those who came before me. Ensuring our privacy is the first step in keeping our secret and our people safe. We mostly shift and run at night when it would be hard to spot us without being seen yourself. In addition, there is an underground running path with various obstacles for everyone's use. Often it is where we teach the young ones to run and navigate the world as a tiger. I must admit, you adapted very quickly."

"I didn't have much of a choice. My tigress came forward to keep me from being raped and kidnapped or killed—I was never sure which. It didn't take a rocket scientist to realize that she was keeping me safe. It was a bit unnerving to say the least, but at the time, I felt I didn't have much of a choice."

"She did keep you safe," he said.

"Yes, she did. And she got me away from you… at least, for a while."

"But only for a while. Remember that, my mate, I will always track you down and bring you home. You are lucky that so much had happened and that I was happy to have you back with me."

"Lucky?" she asked incredulously as they started down the stairs.

He nodded. "The next time you try to escape or evade me, you will find yourself across my lap facing discipline."

Rhys hated the way his deep voice and bold words made the butterflies in her belly take flight. He really was an incredibly sexy and enticing man, and it was hard not to remember what it had been like that night at Baker Street. She wondered again about whether it was advisable to remain with Lars while she hunted down her sister's killer. He seemed as committed to keeping her out of it as she was to be included.

Granted, he had money and resources she didn't, but it was beginning to be a struggle to resist the way her body responded to his proximity and the way he could soothe whatever ached without touching her. There was a kind of magic to the man, but she had no desire to succumb to its seductive serenade.

There was also, she reminded herself, the small

matter of Scotland Yard thinking she was some kind of master art thief and Interpol and the police in Lyon wanting her for questioning in the murder of her sister.

As they reached the bottom, Lars said, "You seem lost in thought."

"Not lost but confused."

"Perhaps I can help clarify what causes you concern."

"You are what causes me concern."

He took her arm, tucking it into his own. "Then there should be nothing confusing. I have claimed you as my mate. We will figure out the answer to the mystery of the Raphael and your sister's killer or killers will be made to answer for their actions."

Rhys thought about telling him he was so wrong about not being the cause of her unease, but felt it was best to let the matter rest. She needed to figure out her next move as well as several more after that before she reminded him she had never agreed to any of this.

At the end of what seemed to be a small passageway from the foot of the stairs to a long, dark tunnel, she could see two sets of rails embedded into the floor and what looked like several small, open subway cars, linked together, waiting for them.

"We can walk or take the tram. The castle is almost three miles away."

"I think I'd rather ride than walk."

"Good choice," he said, smiling as he helped her into the comfortable seat of the tram.

Once everyone from the plane was loaded on board, the vehicle pulled away and moved at a good clip along its track. As they rode, she observed the walking path, the lighting and the way the tunnel seemed to be carved out of solid rock.

"This is amazing," she said, not unimpressed. "I take it one set of rails is from the tunnel to the castle, and the other is from the castle back to the hangar?"

"Yes. What has always fascinated me is the determination, engineering, and hard work it must have taken to create the original tunnels. They were dug by hand, long before man learned how to harness the power of explosives. My ancestors and I have worked continually to make the tunnels safer and easier to use."

"I almost feel like any minute now there's going to be a light show and we'll chug up a steep incline before hurtling down the roller coaster on the other side."

"Don't think it hasn't been thought of, especially in the exercise maze, which was my mother's brainchild. She wanted some place for the children to play and be able to shift without concern. She started the design and creation of the maze when I was small and gradually expanded both the network of tunnels as well as the complexity of the obstacles and ways to find your way from point A to point B. They are monitored by a security staff on the off chance someone loses their way."

"I would think that would be fairly easy to do."

"We do have maps and color guided striping along the floor, but while they are well lit, they are tunnels, so it is easy to get lost."

It didn't take long to traverse the track and have the tram come out into a brightly lit area. Rhys noted that only one man was waiting for them. She'd been dreading being greeted by a line of staff, anxiously awaiting their alpha.

The car pulled to a stop and the tall striking man extended his hand to help her out. Gangsters or not, these men all seemed to have very courtly manners.

"Björn," said Lars, "How is Britt?"

"She is fine, Lars, and anxious to meet our new mistress."

"Is there an old mistress?" quipped Rhys.

"There is not, and you are well aware of that fact," rumbled Lars. "Rhys, this is our second-in-command, Björn. His mate is Britt, and she carries their first child."

"Did you ask her before you knocked her up or just follow your leader's inclination to do as you like without asking the woman involved…" Rhys' snarky comment was cut off when Lars' hand connected sharply with her backside.

"That is enough, Rhys," scolded Lars. "I fear my

mate has been overstressed by the current series of events."

Björn nodded. "I can only imagine, not only becoming one with us, but learning of your sister's death. We were all sorry to hear about that. Interpol spy or not, she was well-liked by those who knew her."

Rhys hadn't expected that sentiment. "Thank you. I have to admit I'm still processing Maeve's murder, and I haven't even begun to deal with the whole 'by the way when I bit you, I turned you into a tiger-shifter.'"

Lars growled.

"She has a point, Lars," said a gorgeous woman with hair that was such a pale blonde, it was almost white. Rhys could detect a slight baby bump, but she seemed in good spirits and completely unafraid of either Björn or Lars. "I'm Britt and you must be Rhys. Welcome to Runestone. I'm sure you're exhausted. Let's get you out of this drafty tunnel and up into the keep. We'll be much more comfortable. Would you like to lie down or take a shower? Björn told me you wouldn't have much with you, so Lars sent me into Visby to buy you some things. I had to guess at the sizes, but I think they're close. If you don't like them, I can return them and get something else."

Rhys had to admire the way Britt ignored both Björn and Lars as she whisked her away.

"You have the most amazing eyes," said Britt.

"Thank you. That was pretty impressive back there."

Britt laughed. "I wasn't sure it would work, but I know Björn wants to talk to Lars." They walked into the foyer where a lovely older woman seemed to be waiting. "Rhys, this is Hilda. She is the one who really runs Runestone. She supervises the entire household staff and is also our master chef."

"I am just a simple cook, as you well know," said Hilda to Britt before turning to Rhys. "I am happy to meet you, Mistress. We have waited a long time for Lars to find his fated mate. I took the liberty of planning meals for the next several days, subject to your approval."

"I'm sure whatever you planned will be delicious and well-received."

"I thought I would make you a tray and bring it up to your chambers. Is there anything in particular you'd like or not like?"

"I had something on the plane so I'm not particularly hungry, but if you could find me a Diet Coke or a beer, I'd be most grateful."

"Thank God," said Britt melodramatically as Björn and Lars emerged. "I was scared you might be one of those prissy Brits who only drink hot tea or wine."

"Blech and blech," laughed Rhys. "I drink either café au lait or black—no in-between—but Diet Coke is my drink of choice."

"Hilda, where did you put Rhys?" asked Britt in a tone that held there was more to the question than might meet the eye. This was confirmed by a low, subtle growl from Björn and Hilda looking between Britt, Lars, and Rhys herself.

"My mate will share my chambers," said Lars in an even voice. "Don't cause trouble Britt. You are not yet so far gone that you might not benefit from your mate's loving hand being applied to your backside."

Rhys held up her hand. "That's fine. I don't need everyone making a fuss. Hilda, if you could bring us up a couple of Diet Cokes, that would be great."

"Yes, Mistress," said Hilda. "I put the things Britt picked up for you in your room."

Britt rolled her eyes. "Sorry. I tried."

"Not to worry. Why don't you show me to Lars' room, and we'll take it from there?"

"Unless you need me," said Lars, "Björn and I will be in my office for a bit. Let someone know if you need anything."

"I'm sure I'll be fine. If you could get me whatever information you can about my sister's murder, I'd appreciate it. I'm especially interested in the medical examiner's report."

"Why not just rest and enjoy yourself tonight?"

"Because I'm not on vacation, Lars. I told you I would work with you to find out who killed my sister and who framed me."

She held her ground and his stare. Lars nodded. "I will either have it sent up or bring it to you myself."

"In that case," Rhys said, turning towards the stairs and linking her arm with Britt's, "I think I'll get out of these clothes and grab a quick shower."

As they got to the top of the stairs, Britt turned toward the left, "Well done. I think we're going to get along famously," she said as she led her down to a set of double doors at the end of the hall.

CHAPTER 17

Lars watched her ascend the stairs with Britt in tow. He wondered if she realized how regal and right she looked doing so.

"I will speak with Britt tonight…"

Lars waved Björn off. "Britt is fine. Rhys wasn't raised as one of us; didn't even know we existed. I'll grant you she's taken to it far more quickly than anyone I've ever known, but she's going to need a friend. Someone she can count on."

"My Britt is far from a model of good behavior."

"Yes and no. She has a tendency to misbehave, but usually only so she's yanking your chain, but I would trust her with my Rhys. I do not believe Rhys will act against us. Her tigress knows her place is at my side; Rhys will settle. I'll see to it that she finds great pleasure in my bed, and we will keep her safe and find whoever is responsible for her sister's death."

"The tigresses may be an issue. News has already spread that she did not give her consent to be turned. I think the only one of our females not pissed at you is Hilda, but then she has doted on you since you were a boy."

Lars smiled fondly. "As I do her. Thank Britt for going into Visby to get Rhys some things."

Björn chuckled. "I'm not so sure you'll be happy when you see the bill. Britt tends to have expensive taste, especially when it is *your* money she is spending."

"What do we know about Mara... Maeve's death?"

"Not a lot. They have listed it as death by misadventure."

"That doesn't tell us much."

"No, but the notes indicate it wasn't garroting or any other means of strangulation, no obvious blows by blunt instruments, no gunshot or stab wounds."

"Then poison?"

"That would be my guess, but there was no indication of that."

"Can we get someone in there? I'd like one of our people to examine the body and get a blood sample if they can," said Lars as he paced in front of the window.

"We can arrange that. What are you thinking?"

Lars turned to stand with his back against the window. It felt good to have the sun shining through on his shoulders. "If it's bratva, there should be an injection site, my guess would be in a fleshy part of the body. The blood work should confirm Ricin. It's become one of their favorite methods. Easy and effective."

"Rhys doesn't really think we were involved does she?"

"I don't think she does—not in her gut, but she's still reeling from Maeve's death and from being turned. Her tigress has a habit of hissing at me down the tether." Lars said the last with a bit of amusement.

"You can sense her tigress when she is human?" Björn was astonished. There were the odd tales here and there about fated mates being able to communicate and recognize each other through their altered selves, but most dismissed the stories as fairytales.

"Not only sense her, but I can see and feel her prowling on the fringes of Rhys' mind. She and Rhys have a somewhat unorthodox relationship."

"Does Rhys have control?"

"As far as I can tell yes. But her tigress had to come forward to save Rhys' life. Rhys is intelligent and instinctive enough that she was able to accept her tigress and shifting as part of her reality. They seem to communicate back and forth."

"That is odd."

Lars grinned. "Rhys informed me if we couldn't do it that way, we'd been doing it wrong."

"And you don't find it alarming that her tigress is so present, for lack of a better term?"

"Considering she kept Rhys alive when I could not, I am inclined to be grateful. Besides, Rhys finds her presence comforting."

"How much trouble do you think she's going to have coming to grips with the fact that she is your mate?"

"We found great pleasure in each other's arms at Baker Street, thus the reason I allowed my tiger's more primitive inclinations to take hold and claim her. I wonder now if he didn't sense the strength of the tigress that laid within her. She is resentful that I, as she sees it, stole her humanity. And yet, I think she also knows somewhere deep down that she is mine and is where she needs to be. I will try to give her time to accept, but I will also teach her to obey, regardless of what she thinks, and I intend to keep her happy and sated."

"Keep in mind without knowing about any of us, she was able to get away from two thugs and outmaneuver us in London. Her sister must have had her set up a way to get out if things went horribly wrong."

"Which they did, and which I take responsibility for. I was so entranced with having found and claimed my fated mate that I did not keep my guard up and keep her safe. She should never have found out about Maeve the way she did. And they made her go into their cold room while they pulled the body out."

"Bastards," snarled Björn.

"It would have been bad enough if she'd had to

identify her on a table in a viewing room. But instead, they dragged her into the autopsy room and pulled her sister out of a drawer. My mate is strong, and they tried to break her. Instead, she turned against them."

"Do you think they believe she did it?"

"Doubtful. I'm not even sure the Yard actually believes the whole art theft accusation, but we need to deal with that as well."

There was a knock on the door and Hilda entered with two frosted bottles of Falcon, one of Sweden's premiere beers. "I thought you might be thirsty," she said.

"Thank you, Hilda. And my mate has all she needs?" asked Lars.

"Yah, Alpha. She is most beautiful, and she and Britt seem to be hitting it off."

Björn laughed. "I'm not sure if that's a good thing or not." Hilda left and Björn continued. "Our man in the Visby police said so far nothing has come across his desk, but he will keep an eye out. And they are ignoring Interpol's request for drone surveillance."

"Do they have any drones left? I know we've taken out three in the past couple of months with those EMP blasts."

"You can't blame them for ignoring Interpol. Those drones are damned expensive and the ones we haven't taken down have shown them nothing. Does Rhys know about the tunnels?"

"In general, which reminds me, let's increase our

security for a while and set guards in the tunnels. I think she realizes we are in a position to help her find Maeve's killer, and maybe even with the stolen Raphael, but unless I have her convinced that she belongs with me before then, I may need to ensure she stays put."

"I don't understand about the theft charge. Do you think someone at Lloyd's has it in for her?"

"No, but do a deep dive on her friend Laura Ashton. I do think the two are connected."

"How so?" asked Björn.

"Unsure, but I don't think it's a coincidence that her sister tried to come at us through our smuggling and art brokering and it's a Raphael that Rhys is accused of stealing."

"Does Rhys have any ideas?"

"I'm sure she does. All she's told me is that she thinks it's some kind of fraud, as the Raphael she was working on was a forgery. She was just about to turn in her final report, but her laptop was stolen with the draft of her findings and all her notes. My guess is her computer at work has been wiped clean or at the very least, those files have disappeared along with the phony Raphael."

"Why don't you get her to give us either the name of the piece or a description. I can let our contacts know we are looking for it and that there is a reward for anyone who leads us to it."

Lars knew that Björn was trying to act in the best

interest of his mate, but he wasn't sure putting out a reward that told the world they were looking for the painting or interested in any information regarding it was the way to go.

"Let's hold off on that. I'd rather not alert anyone behind this that we might have put the two together. Instead, let's follow up on Maeve's death and very quietly tiptoe around the Raphael. I want to make sure we've had nothing to do with this. I don't remember our handling a Raphael, but I want you to make sure."

"I agree. But let me do some nosing around. The more we know about the painting, the better off we'll be. I think, if at all possible, it would be best if we had your mate's expertise."

Lars nodded. "Agreed. It will also make her feel as if she is being included, which she is…"

"But at a safe distance."

"Exactly. And you are right. Her expertise would be invaluable. Anything else while I was gone? What about the Chagall?"

"Both parties are still interested in making the deal and are convinced we had no hand in what went down; they have discovered the mole and dealt with it. For what it's worth, word is you are the one who killed Maeve, so that seems to have satisfied them."

"I imagine my offering to cut our fee in half didn't hurt."

"I think that may have played a part, yes. Does Rhys believe you had a hand in Maeve's death?"

"I don't think so. She thinks I know more than I'm letting on, which I don't, but I do not believe that she thinks that I killed her or gave the order to have her killed. Set up another exchange. This time, let's meet somewhere in the Baltic Sea. Everyone brings their own boat. We meet on ours. That way we'll have an open sight line to any trouble."

"How soon?"

"If they want me present, next week at the earliest. If they will settle for my representative, we can do it this week."

"I can go…"

Lars shook his head. "No. I want to look at who we assign to projects and deals offsite. I now know what it felt like to be parted from my fated mate. Not only do I feel for those of you who have served me so well, I can only imagine what your mates must feel like. Unless absolutely necessary, I prefer to have our soldiers who leave Runestone be unmated."

"Yes, Alpha. My guess is that will be a most welcome change."

"Make sure the clan knows that the only reason is that their alpha is besotted with his own mate. I want it stressed that it has nothing to do with ability or my lack of faith in any of them."

"Do you really want them to know how you feel about her before she has settled?"

"Yes. I don't think it hurts for them to see their alpha as human as they are. Besides, I doubt Rhys is going to be subtle about her feelings."

The two men sat back and went over the remaining business of both the clan and the Berserker Syndicate. With a firm understanding of what Lars wanted, Björn left him to finish up on his own.

Lars spun his large leather office chair around and looked out the enormous window that sat behind his desk. It was surrounded beneath the sill and on either side with an enormous black walnut built in. There had never been a comfortable cushion on the storage bench that ran between the two bookcases, but Lars liked the idea of Rhys being able to curl up in the sunshine in his office within arm's reach.

He wanted to be able to take his mate into seclusion for at least a couple of days. He wanted the opportunity to bind her to him in as many ways as he could. As tactile and responsive as Rhys was, he knew that sex could be a large component of that. The more committed to him that she was, the safer he could keep her, or at least, that's what he tried to tell himself.

The truth was far more selfish and far less complex. He needed her in a way he'd never needed anyone, and he would do whatever it took to ensure she was by his side from now until they crossed into eternity together.

CHAPTER 18

Rhys looked around the room and marveled at its size and furnishings. The bed was an enormous four poster with barley twist spindles she was sure she couldn't fit her hands around. The polished floors had a soft satin sheen and feel to them. The windows were large and allowed light to stream through them. The room was about the size of her entire flat back in London.

"I swear if you added a small kitchenette, this room is bigger and better than my place in London," said Rhys.

Britt smiled. "I was born and raised here at Runestone. I've never had a place that was all my own. Don't get me wrong, I love it here, but sometimes I wonder." She placed her hand on her belly.

"When are you due?"

"Not for another four and a half months. At least

I'm through the morning sickness, which in my case was an all-day sickness. Poor Björn. I swear he suffered more than I did. I was sorry to hear about your sister. I didn't get to spend a lot of time with her, but she seemed like a lot of fun."

Rhys found herself smiling as tears filled her eyes. "She was. And while intellectually I always knew that what she did was dangerous, I never expected her to be killed in the line of duty. At least I hope that's why she was murdered."

"Why do you say that?"

"Because if not, because then her death is linked to whatever is happening to me..." Rhys said, sinking down onto the edge of the bed.

"Listen to me," Britt said fiercely as she joined her. "You are *not* responsible for her death. Whoever killed her is responsible for whatever reason they killed her. It really doesn't matter if it is because of her work for Interpol or because someone is trying to set you up. The only person responsible is the one who murdered her, and Lars will see that they pay."

"It's not always that easy. A lot of time the loss of an agent is seen as collateral damage and part of the cost of doing business."

"Maybe by her employers but not by her family."

"We were all that was left of our family."

"Nothing could be further from the truth. Everyone who knew her liked her. That's why her being a spy hurt people. They felt as if they knew her, and she lied to them. I think that isn't true."

"She worked for Interpol and her job was to bring Lars down."

"Pfft," said Britt dismissively. "That may be how it started, but I think she was having second thoughts. I think she revealed a part of herself to us that perhaps only you knew. I don't think in the end she could have done it. I think she would have left Interpol rather than destroy us."

"Did she know who or what you or we are?"

"No. I think she was beginning to suspect there was something different about us, but the jump to us being tiger-shifters is pretty huge. And you have a family now—a rather large and noisy one. That means what happens to you happens to us all. Those responsible for Mara… wait, her real name was Maeve, right?" Rhys nodded. "Those responsible for Maeve's death will be held to account. If they do not face the human justice system, they will face Lars' judgment and he is not one to allow his people—his family—to be killed."

"I hope so. The idea of someone having killed her and getting away with it is more than I can handle." Rhys shook her head.

"What?"

"I can feel my tigress in the back of my mind. She has some very definite thoughts on how to make them pay—very violent, very bloody ways."

Britt laughed. "I'll bet she does. You seem to be doing remarkably well for someone who knew nothing about our kind and is now one of us."

"I'm not sure I'm actually one of you."

"You are," Britt said, patting her hand. "You may not have accepted that, and Lars should be punched in the nose for having turned you without your consent, but men in love often do foolish things."

Rhys snorted. "Lars isn't in love with me. I'll grant you we had a pretty intense connection at Baker Street, but I never confuse lust with love."

"We may have to agree to disagree. Lars is a strong-willed man. For him to disregard one of our most closely held tenets regarding consent from a human to be turned, there had to be more there than mere lust. He wouldn't lose control… that's wrong. Lars doesn't ever lose control like that. Ignoring one of our most sacred tenets was an act of will. Unless he was sure you are his fated mate, he never would have done it. But that doesn't change things. Are you all right with what happened?"

Rhys took a deep breath, trying to get a handle on the turbulent emotions that seemed to swirl all around her. "That's a difficult question to answer honestly. The whole tiger thing is interesting."

"'Interesting?' I don't think I have ever heard it called 'interesting.'"

"It's the only word I can come up with. She saved my life. If she hadn't come forward and initiated the first change, I'm not sure how long it would have taken me to try to shift. But I'm still angry at Lars for thinking he can just swoop into my life and throw my world into chaos. A part of me knows not all of this is his fault, but I'm still pretty pissed at him."

"I understand that; I'm not sure I wouldn't feel the same, but I would point out, it sounds like your tigress saved your life so there is that."

"There is indeed. There's also the fact that I enjoy her presence. Lars says she and I have a different relationship from most of you." Rhys gave a little laugh. "I told him the rest of you are doing it wrong."

"Just so you know, you are not alone. You are one of us now. I'll let you get settled in. Björn and I are at the other end of the hall, and if you need anything, the retro looking phone rings down to Hilda. She'll get you anything you need."

"What if I want to leave here?"

Taking a deep breath, Britt took her hands in her own. "I hope you won't. I hope at least you'll stay until we know what's going on and know you will be safe. Then if you feel you need to be gone from us, there are a number of tigresses who will help you—myself included. I know our ways can seem archaic at first and sometimes the men are a bit overbearing and almost always territorial and possessive, but they mean well. For the most part, it works. But if you can't be happy here, we are your family and we will see that you are where you need to be to thrive."

"Even if it means invoking your alpha's wrath?"

Britt nodded. "Even if. Just promise me you'll think about staying, at least until we know more, if not until we know you will be safe."

"Thank you, Britt. My thoughts are such a mass of confusion, I'm having trouble remembering my own name."

Britt rose gracefully from the bed and headed back into the hall. She did not lock the door behind her. Rhys wandered over to the window and marveled at the view. She could see the Baltic Sea in the distance, but between Runestone and the shore, was a vast expanse of green space and what appeared to be a tiny village of some sort. She didn't think it was Visby, at least not from this window.

The door opened and she sensed rather than heard Lars enter the room. For a large man, he moved... well, like a predatory cat. He walked up to stand behind her and placed his hands lightly on her arms. The touch was at once electrifying and soothing. Rhys allowed herself the luxury of leaning back against him and closing her eyes, savoring the connection between them, feeling his strength and reassurance—all without saying a word.

"That isn't Visby, is it?"

"No, that's Runestad. Technically, it is part of Runestone. It is a small fishing village where those of our people who make a living fishing keep their boats, offload their catch, etc. We also have business interests in Visby as well as other parts of Sweden and around the world."

"So, you have varied interests? Not just illegal art?"

Again, she felt more than heard a deep chuckle. "We don't make a lot on stolen art or brokering deals. It's more of a hobby. The real money in smuggling is to be made in booze and tobacco products."

Rhys realized he was, at least in part, teasing her. "Good to know," she quipped. "I'm not sure I will stay with you."

"Forever or just in this room? Not that you have a choice in either."

"Does it matter? I mean, are you willing to accept my decision?"

"No," he said honestly. "But it at least lets me know where we're starting from."

"You can't think what you did to me is okay."

"What I think is that I simply moved past the preliminaries and enacted the inevitable. You are my fated mate. What's more, I believe you know that."

"What if I don't want to be?"

"Why would you not? Our connection at Baker Street was intense. I can keep you safe and provide whatever you want from this life. The only mistake I made was in not reining in my tiger's instinctive need to mark and claim you as mine. I did what I knew to be right—as I always do. Claiming you in the manner I did was instinctive and inescapable."

"But you agree you should have asked me."

"I agree that most would have sought your acquiescence, but it has never been mandatory, at least not for an alpha claiming his mate. I am the Winter Tiger. My word is law. I allowed the ecstasy I found in your arms to make me complacent. I should have ensured you didn't get away. Had I done so, those men who tried to harm you would never have been in a position to do so. You could have been lost to me because I allowed myself to become seduced by the moment and dropped my guard. A guard you should be able to trust will always be there to keep you safe. I will not allow that to happen again."

Rhys shoved her elbow into his solar plexus and spun around, kicking him in the shins when he released her. "God, you're an insufferable ass."

Breaking away from him, she sprinted across the room, threw open the door and called her tigress forward. As the sparkling colors and flashes of light swirled and shimmered all around her, she heard Lars roar and could feel his anger surging down the tether. She might not be able to get away or even keep him from dragging her to his bed, but by God, she would make him work for it and he would understand her feelings on the matter.

She hit the ground as her tigress, bowling Björn over as he raced down the hall, hearing Britt call. "You're better off staying out of the tunnels. They're a maze if you don't know them."

"Britt, that's enough!" roared Björn as Rhys galloped down the stairs.

A surge of freedom and power flowed through her body, filling every cell with a feeling of wellbeing. Even as enraged as she was at the situation Lars had put her in—not all by himself, but he had a large hand in it, she could appreciate the gift he had given her. Rhys charged towards the closed door, thinking to crash through one of the sidelights on either side. Lars roared again, which only urged her tigress to find more speed. The door opened to admit someone just as she reached the foyer. Before the poor man could react to what was happening, Rhys had raced past him and was outside.

She ran for the moat, allowing her tigress' sense of smell to guide her. Lars might have been right about swimming it as a human, but she believed her tigress would see them across. Unlike most cats, tigers loved the water and were powerful swimmers. Rhys ran, using every bit of speed and muscle that her tigress possessed to get them to the edge of the water. She could hear Lars galloping after them.

Rhys sprang into a large fountain in the courtyard and pushed off with her back feet, sending various pieces flying and slamming into Lars. She hit the cobblestones of the bailey, noting their well-worn texture. Out the gate and onto the grass—its cool, soft texture a marked contrast to that of the heated, hard texture of the stone that had been underfoot lining the driveway. The grass was a bit more slippery, but the earth beneath her feet allowed her to find traction.

Feeling her muscles ripple as she ran, she focused on her target, which was becoming closer with each powerful stride. She didn't hesitate as she approached the bank; Rhys put on a burst of speed and leaped off the bank, stretching her body to gain as much distance as she could in the air before hitting the water.

Splashing into the icy water, she realized her fur insulated her from the cold wet tendrils that tried to grasp at her. Lars roared again. She glanced back over her shoulder to see him snarling and pacing along the bank of the moat—trying, she supposed, to decide whether to slide down it or take the big plunge as she had. There was something amusing when he opted to slide down the slippery slope and into the moat. He began paddling to try and catch her, but his hesitation had cost him, Rhys now had a substantial lead.

Gaining the other bank, she did not stop to shake herself. Rhys allowed instinct and outrage to propel her forward. She had to admit that being able to shapeshift had some advantages. There was no way she would have been able to run at this speed for this long as a human. She wasn't even breathing hard. The longer and faster she ran, the easier it was for her. The wind blowing over her coat was drying and warming her.

Rhys did not delude herself into believing she

could get away from him; she wasn't even sure she wanted to. No, this run was about not being manipulated and about getting Lars to acknowledge he couldn't just make plans about her future without consulting her. Rhys ran for the trees, both to give her cover from anyone trying to spy on them from overhead, as well as innately understanding it would be easier to lose Lars and/or outrun him in the woods. Out in the open on a flat plane, he could easily catch her. He was bigger, stronger, and in better shape.

Rhys charged past the edge of the forest, leaping over downed trees and switching direction—always moving forward, but not in a straight line, more of an erratic zig zag diagonal. She had to admit, she hadn't thought this plan through, but for now she just needed to make her point.

Why was that important to her? Why ensure Lars understood she would not be dictated to and that he could not make unilateral decisions about her future? If she was committed to leaving him, did it really matter? Wasn't it easier to simply allow him to believe he had what he wanted until she was able to find her sister's killer and clear her own name? Was she actually beginning to envision a future with Lars?

CHAPTER 19

Rhys continued to make her way to the far side of the forest where she encountered the wall that surrounded the estate. As a tigress it wouldn't be all that difficult to climb the wall, but then what? She had no idea what lay beyond. If she scaled the wall during daylight, she could be easily spotted. She didn't fancy spending the rest of her life in a zoo, or worse yet in a lab as some kind of biological science experiment.

She stopped and stilled her breathing, listening intently. She could hear movement, but it sounded neither close nor headed her way. Perhaps her best bet would be to find a place to hide. Rhys moved silently through the trees and found a long dead, fallen tree that had a natural hollow. She removed some of the debris and laid down, curling into a ball to consider her options and wait until nightfall. Then if she decided to leave Runestone, she wouldn't be as easily spotted.

If she chose to leave, being seen was the least of her worries. If she shifted back, she would be naked. Worse than that, she had no money, no identification and both Interpol and Scotland Yard were looking for her. Not her best plan. But that begged the question, what did she want? Did she want to be out on her own? Someone had killed her sister—a sister who was a trained agent of Interpol. And someone had tried to come after her in London.

Rhys had to admit she was safer with Lars and his people than out on her own. He did seem committed to finding those who had killed Maeve and if not bring them to justice, at least make them pay for what they had done. She began to question why she had reacted to his presence in the master's chambers the way she did. He hadn't really done anything wrong, had he? All she'd known was that in that moment, she'd had to get away, had to exert her independence.

Anger and fear had compelled her to act. But anger and fear about what and directed at who? Lars had done nothing wrong, if you didn't include turning her into a shapeshifter. The elation she had felt when she'd eluded him was beginning to fade and she realized her behavior had been uncalled for. She didn't normally go around physically attacking people.

Normally, she didn't give into her temper or act without thinking—was that a byproduct of becoming a tiger-shifter?

Funny, now that she was still and quiet, she could see the sense in remaining with Lars and his people—at least until she found Maeve's killer and cleared her name. The problem with staying with Lars would be that he would expect her to sleep with him. She had to admit from her point of view, sleeping with Lars—more specifically, having sex with Lars—was not a bad idea. What left a bad taste in her mouth was that if she wasn't planning to stay, allowing him to assume otherwise didn't seem fair.

Lars was a man of incredible sensuality, carnality, and ability. One night with him had taught her that. She felt arousal bloom in her nether regions as the primal, almost feral side of her psyche began to crave his touch. Visions of nights spent in his arms in that enormous bed filled her mind, so much so that she failed to hear his approach until it was almost too late. The snap of the twig and his scent wafting to her on the breeze warned her of his presence.

Springing to her feet—all four of them—she launched herself over the top of the log and began to run a more direct path back to the castle. Lars roared and thundered after her, leaping and bringing his heavy body down on hers, driving her to the ground. He grabbed the back of her neck in his powerful jaws and pinned her to the ground. There was no doubt in either of their minds who the victor would be in a contest of strength.

He shook her by the scruff of the neck. Rhys willed her body to go limp in submission, but that didn't seem to satisfy him. He shook her by the scruff of her neck and then dragged her back to the fallen tree where she had curled into a ball. She felt the cold mist and electricity of the shimmer as Lars changed from tiger to man and shook her again. It wasn't as effective, but she felt his anger flowing freely down the tether to her. Unprepared for the onslaught of raw emotion, Rhys felt overwhelmed.

"Shift," he commanded, his blue eyes flashing anger and lust in the same instant.

His tone indicated that he would brook no disobedience. Her tigress might be strong and willing to taunt him from a distance, but face-to-face with his dominance, she retreated in a swirl of color and light and was gone, leaving Rhys naked on her knees before him. His cock confronted her and without thinking she licked her lips and started to lean forward.

Lars tangled his fingers in her luscious mane and pulled upward. Rhys had no choice but to follow her hair. He didn't stop pulling until she was standing on her tiptoes in front of him. His eyes roamed down the length of her body, taking in her full breasts with her pebbled nipples. From there he gazed down to her belly, her hips and her naked sex. Rhys felt herself blush as his gaze left no doubt in her mind that he believed her to be his.

Without a word, Lars sat down on the fallen tree, using the fist in her hair to haul her over his hard, muscular, naked thighs. His cock had responded to her proximity by becoming fully engorged and now throbbed beneath her belly. A memory of what it was to feel that cock thrust up as he began to pound inside her flashed across her mind, making her tigress purr in sensual pleasure.

'You are no help, whatsoever,' she said to her tigress.

Lars wrapped his arm around her waist, securing her in place, and ran his other hand across her ass, caressing it. Her brain only had a fraction of a second to register the sharp updraft from his hand as it rose before it crashed back down on her bare backside. The sound of his hand as he spanked her ricocheted through the trees like a gunshot. It didn't take more than six or seven smacks before the warm heat that had initially been imparted began to spread with an uncomfortable fire that moved not just across her bottom but throughout her system.

How dare he spank her? Granted, she'd elbowed and kicked him, shifting and fleeing the castle like some simpering damsel in distress from the evil overlord. But she didn't simper, and he was not evil. Resentment gave way to arousal as the emotion that flowed down the tether turned from anger to lust. Rhys kicked her legs, trying desperately to free herself and fight off the ambush of her response to his dominance.

Again and again, his hand landed a resounding blow, covering her entire ass and turning her upturned rump into two heated globes. She tried to remain stoic and not respond in any way, but Lars was a man, a trained Dom, an alpha male bent on imposing his will, and she was almost helpless to resist him. Every instinct told her that if she capitulated, the spanking would be curtailed and then perhaps he would offer her comfort in the form of sex, but Rhys wasn't yet willing to give over.

~

Rhys' resistance should have fueled his anger. Instead, it turned anger and concern to lust and need. Her bottom was turning the most enticing shade of red, and Lars was sure his mate had not been spanked in a very, very long time. Her soft skin was sensitive and responded in the most alluring way.

She was not afraid of him—hadn't been afraid in their room, either. She had lashed out in frustration and resentment. He could sense she had realized the foolishness of her escape, but he meant to bring home the idea that she was his, would remain at his side and learn to obey him. He continued to swat her beautiful bottom, enjoying the way her cheeks had just the right amount of bounce to them.

Lars realized when he'd taken a look at her body that she was, in his opinion, perhaps the most beautiful thing he'd ever laid eyes on, and considering he lived under the aurora borealis, that was saying something. An hourglass figure, long legs and a fit body that was still shapely and soft in all the right spots. She had hips a man could grasp when he wanted to hold her in place as he took her from behind, and her buttocks would be a nice handful when he settled himself between her thighs.

He inhaled her intoxicating scent and grinned as her arousal grew to meet his own. His cock was hard and throbbed against her belly, wanting to reclaim her wet heat as it had done the first time in London. Her body was responding to the spanking, the dominance, and his feelings of longing and need he let flow through the tether to her.

Pushing her legs apart with his hand, he slapped her wet sex, making a splatting sound as she cried out. She might be able to remain stoic during a regular spanking, but she wasn't used to having her sex spanked. She ground down against his leg, trying to find relief for what he was sure was a swollen little nub.

When she tried to close her thighs, he growled,

swatted her lower lips even harder, and forced them apart again. Her cunt exposed to his gaze, he allowed pure, primal lust and need to flow down the tether. He would overwhelm her not only physically, but emotionally as well. This time when he claimed her, she would have no doubt about her place or who was dominant.

Lars began spanking her again in a slower, more rhythmic fashion but with equal intensity—one slap to each of her cheeks and one between her legs. Slowly and methodically, he ramped up her arousal as she began to anticipate each blow—he could swear her labia shivered after each swat to her ass, waiting for the slap to her sex.

"You're wet, my beautiful tigress. Do you understand who your master is?"

"You are not my master," she gasped as he landed one-two-three more swats to her bottom and sex.

"We both know that isn't true. You will not run from me. Each time you do, I will find you and each time I have to discipline you, I will make it worse than the time before."

He ceased spanking her and allowed his fingers to delve between her legs, parting her labia and sliding along the opening to her core, making her moan. He cupped her sex in his large hand, giving it a gentle, possessive squeeze. The tips of his fingers almost caressed her clit—almost, but not quite. Lars began to move his hands in ever-quickening circles around her clit until he pinched it between his thumb and forefinger sending her over the abyss into a short, sharp orgasm that made her cry out as her cream coated his hand.

CHAPTER 20

Lars stood, fisting her hair and positioning her so that she was bent face down over the tree trunk he'd been sitting on. He held her down as he stepped between her legs. Surely, he didn't mean to fuck her out here like this, did he? The head of his cock as it parted her labia told her that was just what he planned to do. She tried to get up or squirm away, but he had her pinned down and meant to take what he obviously thought of as his.

Guiding his cock to its intended target, he pressed forward, her inner walls softening and accepting him as he began to plunder her wet pussy. It was just as she remembered, and she was falling prey to his mesmerizing ability to bring her pleasure. His cock felt as though small nubs were raised all along it, providing a new sensation that enhanced her already considerable arousal and need. As he pulled back, it was as if those nubs became little spikes or barbs. Rhys cried out as they scored her sensitive flesh.

"That is what it is to be a tigress and the fated mate to the alpha of our clan. You will come to know the feeling of my barbs well, my mate."

Over and over, he thrust into her, the nubs grazing the delicate tissue of her channel and then raking that same space as he drew back. Thrust after thrust he plundered her pussy, his hard hips and thighs slamming into her well-spanked ass reminding her that she was being punished by her mate. Her tigress yowled and hissed as he exerted his dominance.

Never in her life had she felt anything like this. Pleasure and pain morphed into one as Lars pounded into her, growling with need and desire. He pounded into her with greater intensity as she pushed back against him. Their coupling was powerful, frenzied and primal. His dick stretched her pussy as again and again he hammered her with his enormous cock. She'd never taken a man of his length or girth before and she was surprised that it even fit, much less felt as amazing as it did. It was as if her pussy had been molded to accommodate him.

She felt his plunging rod swelling, twitching, the barbs digging in until finally they seemed to sink into her as if to anchor her pussy to his cock. She felt her body tremble as he reached under her to pinch her clit again, sending her over the edge of the abyss into a freefall of orgasmic sensation and submission. Lars had claimed his prize in more ways than one. Deep inside her, he began to flood her pussy with his seed, his hips bumping her painful backside as her pussy contracted all up and down his length, rhythmically milking it for every last bit of what he had to give her.

Before she could utter a word, the barbs released and Lars drew back, uncoupling from her before lifting her up and tossing her over his shoulder. He stalked back towards the castle, his captured prize hanging upside down, bouncing along with her red backside on display and his cum dripping down the inside of her thighs. He stopped at the edge of the forest, setting her down only long enough to pull on jeans someone had left for him.

Did that mean someone had seen them fucking or heard her as she yowled in response to his primitive, feral way of subduing her? Rhys wondered if it was possible for her to simply wither into nothing or have a hole open up in the ground so she could sink into it. But nothing so easy or less mortifying was to be. Lars lifted her back off the ground, hitching her up on his shoulder, ignoring the clothes that had been left for her lying on the ground next to his.

"You can't take me back to Runestone like this," she snarled, provoking a swat to her exposed backside.

"I rather think I can."

He stalked across the open ground back to the moat. She wondered how he planned to get them across. She got her answer as he stepped down onto a tied-up boat. Whoever had left the clothes had also left them another way across than the drawbridge. Once on the boat he set her on her feet, his hand going to the top of her head and pressing down until she was kneeling. Lars started the engine and guided the boat across the moat at an almost leisurely pace. On the other side, he neither helped her to her feet nor hoisted her over his shoulder. He simply tangled his fingers in her hair and dragged her up the embankment. She had no choice but to follow along behind him. At the top of the levee, he turned, putting his shoulder into her middle and standing up, leaving her dangling over his shoulder once again.

Lars carried her back to the castle, up the wide exterior steps, through the front door and then up the main staircase from the foyer, down the hall and into their room before tossing her onto the bed. Rhys winced. That spanking might have spiked her arousal, but it had been meant to punish her and it hurt. The smirk on his face let her know he recognized that his point had been made.

"The next time you think to behave like a nasty tempered she-cat instead of the proud tigress you are, I will spank your pretty bottom in front of the entire clan before carrying you to our bed to fuck you hard enough that your yowling rattles the doors and windows. Do you understand me?"

Rhys was afraid if she tried to speak, she'd burst into tears so merely nodded.

"Answer me," he thundered.

"Yes, Sir."

"Master," he snapped.

"Yes, Master."

"Better," he growled, his anger beginning to abate. "You could have been seen by those who would harm us. We never run as tigers out in the open like that during the daylight. You will never do it again, else your tigress' coat won't be the only thing sporting stripes. Understood?"

"Yes, Master."

He nodded as he picked up the house phone. "Hilda? Yah, she is fine. She won't be sitting comfortably for a bit, but then I plan to have her spending most of the time on her belly or on her back. Tell Björn I am taking my mate into seclusion for a few days. I would appreciate you leaving our meals on a tray in the hall. Just knock when you leave them. If Rhys decides to behave herself, she might get to eat them while they are still warm."

Something about the way he casually informed his housekeeper that he meant to keep her in his bed and have his way with her repeatedly set her teeth. *Have his way? Did I just think 'have his way?' What am I—some heroine in one of the romance novels I don't let anyone know I read?* Lars didn't 'have his way' with her; he fucked her —long, hard, and seemingly often. Maeve had always given her such a hard time about the books she enjoyed.

Lars was nothing like the Viking heroes in the books she liked to read. Oh, he might look the part, but they were noble and honorable. Rhys brought her thoughts to a screeching halt—was he really that different? Sure, he was a gangster, but somehow, she knew he wasn't a killer—at least not a cold-blooded one.

It seemed to Rhys she had two choices: she could give into her primal desires and submit, or she could show him her tigress was a match for him, if not physically then in spirit. Much as she wanted to feel him buried inside her, she believed that she needed to show him she was his equal. He might be dominant, but that didn't mean she was any less than him.

Lars turned back to her. "What do you have to say for yourself?"

"Me? You're the asshole that started this," she snarled, refusing to back down.

"Me?" he accused. "You're the one who elbowed me and then raced off in broad daylight. If you don't have a care for yourself, did you not think about your people?"

"My people? They're not my people. They're yours. And you started this whole thing back in London when you bit me…"

"I claimed you," he growled.

"You fucking bit me and made me into a tiger-shifter without bothering to even inform me, much less obtaining my consent to be made one."

"I was under the impression that you and your tigress got along well."

"We do, and I'm not saying it's the worst thing that ever happened to me…"

"Then what are you so angry about?" he said, frowning.

The look on his face was pure confusion as he ran his hands through his hair. He turned away from her and walked to the window before turning back and leaning against the windowsill. Staring at the ground, he exhaled before looking back at her.

"I would point out," he started in a modulated tone, "that had you not left the bed we shared in London, I would have explained."

"But you wouldn't have asked me, would you?" she queried in a calmer tone.

"By the time you woke, I had already claimed you." He shook his head. "You integrated your tiger so swiftly; it is sometimes difficult to remember she hasn't always been part of you."

"What choice did I have? Those men were going to rape me and then either kidnap or kill me. Allowing her to come forward was my only means of escape."

He smiled ruefully. "Don't think it escapes my

notice that had you been where I put you, you would never have been in danger. I knew you were my fated mate, and for me, there was no question that I would claim you. Your sweet submission at Baker Street lulled me into believing there was no need for concern. I shouldn't have slept so contentedly or deeply. I should have scooped you up and left the city with you in my arms. Knowing I finally had you…"

"But you didn't…"

"I did. You refuse to acknowledge that you knew it as well. Most shifters are raised knowing there is a chance they have a fated mate. Alphas are generally born knowing her scent so that when we find her, we can exert our dominance and claim her."

"I didn't think I was submitting to you for anything other than an intimate encounter. I am never, ever going to be one of those women who takes pleasure in submitting. I respect the hell out of those who do, but I'm not one of them. I find peace while I'm doing it, but it's never been more than a way to get out of my own head to heighten my sexual pleasure."

"Is that because you never found a truly worthy Dom—someone who was man enough?"

Now, it was her turn for a rueful smile. For some reason his throwing her words back in her face didn't rankle her. In fact, Rhys was touched to know he remembered.

"Maybe. But maybe I don't want that as a lifestyle

twenty-four/seven. Maybe I just want it for sex; I don't think that's how your clan operates."

"No; it is not. Males are dominant and females are submissive to their mates. And everyone submits to the alpha…"

"That would be you," she said, trying to keep from grinning or relaxing. Rhys did note that while she could feel the tether that stretched between them, Lars was not trying to use it to further his cause.

"Yah," he said. "That would be me. It is not safe for you. I do not think those who confronted you in your flat or those who killed Maeve are done."

Rhys had to take a step back, feeling behind her for the wall. It was solid, being built of brick more than a thousand years before. "You think I'm an actual target?"

"You don't?" he asked, coming up off the windowsill and crossing the room to her.

Lars extended his hand to her and without thinking, she placed her hand in his. He drew her across the room, sitting down in a large wingback chair and gently pulling her into his lap.

"I thought they wanted to hurt me in London. Of course, later I found they'd killed my sister and were trying to frame me. At first, I didn't think the two were connected."

"It is the explanation that makes the most sense, if you accept that I didn't kill Maeve or order it done."

"I don't think you did… oh God, Lars, they killed my sister. My sister is dead."

Rhys felt something inside her break. Things had been moving so fast and she'd been running so hard, doing whatever she needed just to stay whole. But she wasn't, Maeve was dead, and she wondered if she might ever be whole again.

CHAPTER 21

Rhys' entire body trembled as the weight of her sister's murder finally settled on her. Lars'd been pretty sure she had managed to compartmentalize it. Her body collapsed against him as she instinctively sought his comfort. She reached out to him along the bonding link, not knowing or having the words she needed to express her grief.

Lars wrapped his arms around her, pulling her close and purring to her as he stroked her hair and down her back, holding her hand as she began to break apart and tears began to fall. Lars knew there were those who would think he had not punished her enough for her disobedient display, but all he wanted to do was let her know she was safe and was not alone. He didn't need to talk. He just needed to let her be and know that he was with her.

"It's all right, sweetheart, I'm here. You are not

alone and those who took your sister from you will pay—one way or another."

His soothing tone and stroking seemed to allow her to cast away her defenses and rest within his embrace, seeking solace. At first her posture had been rigid, and she held herself away from him, but little by little he shifted them both until she was fully ensconced in his lap and had no choice but to allow her body to relax against his. He even managed to keep his cock from thumping up against her. He knew she needed to rest; he knew they needed to find common ground where they could come together and move forward. But his cock thought getting back inside her was the best idea of all. It wasn't that he didn't agree with his unruly member, but he was also realizing Rhys wouldn't be dictated to, and she was hurting. He needed to give her what she *needed,* not what he *wanted*.

He knew she believed she had a point. And perhaps from her point of view, he should have asked her, but he hadn't. There had been no need. She was his fated mate and one way or another, he had meant to claim her and had done so in the most expedient manner available. The fact that it angered her really didn't make much difference. Even if he could have foreseen all that followed, he wasn't sure he would have changed anything.

Lars had to admit, if he had handled things differently, he might not be fighting the battle she seemed determined to wage with him. From her viewpoint, he should have asked her. Hell, she probably thought he should have been straight with her about who and what he was and then asked for her consent to be turned. But he hadn't.

He told himself it was because he'd known she was his fated mate. She was his to claim by right as alpha of his clan. And for some females—human or tigress—knowing that he had chosen them would be enough. There was a time when cavemen had not had to follow such niceties. They found their mate, dragged them back to the cave, took them beneath their furs and procreated.

But the time of the caveman had long since passed. It didn't really matter; he was pretty sure it wouldn't have worked for her then, either. She was not going to accept her place at his side without some kind of conciliatory gesture on his part. Neither Rhys nor her tigress was willing to back down if he kept forcing the issue. Cornered predators were always the most dangerous. He was willing to admit that perhaps his treatment of her had been a bit high-handed. Lars understood the art of warfare. It was all well and good to win the battle as he had in the forest, but they would need to find a way to move forward together if Rhys was to truly settle, accept her place at his side and be happy. He realized that her happiness, not just her submission, was important to him.

Lars could sense her tigress prowling at the edge

of her mind. At first, she paced restlessly, ears back and tail swishing slowly back and forth, hissing and snarling at him and his intrusion into the space she shared with Rhys. Little by little as Rhys cried, her tigress began to settle, sensing that Lars was no threat and only sought to give them both solace.

He had never heard of anyone whose altered self was so much a part of them. It seemed Rhys and her tigress were connected in a far different and more profound way. While he knew his tiger was there, ready to spring forth if Lars needed him, he was always just out of reach in the darkest corners of Lars' psyche. Rhys' tigress, on the other hand, seemed to dwell just at the fringes of her conscious mind.

Rhys settled against him, and the heart-wrenching sobs trickled to silent tears and then abated all together as her breathing deepened, evening out as she fell asleep. When he thought about it and as he opened himself to her emotions, he could feel her grief, exhaustion, and confusion. She was unsure who to trust or what to do next. She would need him to lead her so that she emerged at the other end healed and ready to embrace her new life.

When the soft knock on the door came, Lars called quietly for the tray to be brought in. He was ravenous, but his mate needed sleep more than anything. For now, she seemed most content snuggled in his lap.

"Just put the tray here," he said quietly, "and bring me a blanket. She is worn out and is finally resting."

Hilda smiled benignly at him. "Yah, Alpha. Would you like me to bring something else back that will be tasty regardless of the temperature? She will need to eat."

"Thank you, Hilda. I appreciate your concern." He smiled as he took the blanket from her, laying it gently over Rhys' soft and tranquil body.

"She is home now, Alpha. She will heal here; we will all help her."

Lars nodded. At least his people understood. Now, he just needed to make Rhys understand.

"Rhys is not yet ready for seclusion. Tell Björn I am available if he hears anything or needs me. But please close the door and tell those who need to talk to me to be quiet. I don't want her awakened."

"You are truly her fated mate."

"As she is mine."

Lars held her and let her sleep, purring to her whenever he sensed she or her tigress were beginning to regain consciousness. A gentle tap on the door and Björn entered.

"Not what I expected," Björn said.

"Not what I had in mind when I hauled her in here. But as you often tell me, when you are gifted with a fated mate, you adjust your priorities. I realized I hadn't seen her cry or even express sorrow at losing Maeve, and I knew she'd been far too preoccupied with staying alive and free when she wasn't with me. Did anyone see her when she was running?"

"Other than our people? No."

"Make sure they understand she is new to being a shifter and that I explained nothing to her. She has been chastised for her behavior."

Björn chuckled quietly. "The evidence of that was on full display when you brought her back from her little run."

"As far as she is concerned, she had cause."

"Do you agree?"

"No, but I'm not sure if it matters whether I agree. Tell me something, do you ever connect with Britt's tigress?"

"Of course. We run together and wrestle…"

"No. I mean can you sense her at the edge of Britt's mind."

"No," Björn said slowly, shaking his head. "I know that she is there, just as my tiger is always with me…"

"That's the thing, Rhys' tigress isn't in the dim, dark corners. She's on the fringe; when I reach down the tether, I can feel her and see her in my mind's eye."

"How extraordinary. Britt knows a lot of the legends of our people. Let me ask her to do some research. It will give her something to do that isn't too taxing."

Lars chuckled. "You do know tigresses have been

giving birth since time immemorial. You do not have to coddle her."

"Ha. This from the tiger who ran down his mate and brought her back with him naked with a bright red bottom and his seed dripping down her thigh. The same tiger who stormed up the staircase with her, boldly intimating his intention to use her in a less than gentle manner. You just wait until it is Rhys who carries your child. It is far different than watching others. Besides, Britt is good at that sort of thing and is already inordinately fond of your mate."

"I would be curious to know if there is any mention of it made in the scrolls or even the sagas. Have we learned anything new?"

"Her friend Laura has disappeared as well. Gave notice to Lloyds saying she had a family emergency and needed to leave immediately for Canada."

"Does she have family in Canada?"

"No. York. A brother from whom she is estranged. I've reached out to Drummond as he's the closest to see what he can find out."

"You don't think it's a straight up theft or fraud, do you?"

"No. If that was all, why kill Maeve? Why involve Maeve at all? Why even bring a forgery to Lloyds for Rhys to identify and then frame her."

"I agree. I believe the two—the theft/fraud and Maeve's murder are connected, but how?"

"Uncertain. But I can't help but believe it has

something to do with you. I've also reached out to Anders Jensen. He has contacts in Paris, which is the most likely place to fence the painting, as well as to Drummond, to check with those at Scotland Yard. Apparently, he has a connection to them."

"Good. Express my thanks to both. Also let Joshua Knight know we may need to be in London or the surrounding area. He can be territorial on his best days and with the bratva trying to test if they can make inroads in the UK…"

"I know. The damn Cosa Nostra is going to need to take sides less they find themselves with no side at all."

"Reach out to Roman Genovese to see if he can give you a feeling of which way the wind is blowing."

"Why would the Cosa Nostra be involved with the bratva? I thought they were mortal enemies with both the Russian and Albanian mobs."

"Normally they are, which is why it's worrisome they haven't made some kind of declaration in support of our allies in Great Britain and Ireland."

"Do you think the bratva are involved with either the theft or the murder?"

"Fine art is not normally something the bratva are interested in, but they excel at murder. Do we have the postmortem on Maeve?"

"No, but it should be here in the morning. I asked them specifically to look for an injection site."

"Good. Those bastards love that shit. They love

knowing that the person doesn't die immediately and that there is no cure. It's also a particularly nasty way to die and most times the person doesn't even feel ill, at least not immediately. By the time they know they're sick, it's too late."

"As soon as I have the report, I'll bring it to you. Are you planning to sit there all night with her curled up in your lap?"

"If need be. Both she and her tigress are asleep. It is what they both need the most. I will sit here and hold her until she wakes."

Björn chuckled softly. "And you accuse me of coddling Britt. When your mate carries your child in her belly, you're going to be a basket case, and God help us when she goes into labor." Lars growled at him. "Growl all you want, but if your tigress is as fierce as she appears to be, you two are going to be quite entertaining."

Knowing Björn was more likely right than not, Lars chuckled as well. "Perhaps. But for now, I'm more concerned with keeping her safe and making those who murdered her sister pay."

"Once we know, should we simply kill them?"

"No. I want to make sure we know everything they do and then I will let Rhys have a say. After all, it was her sister."

Björn's mobile trilled and he stepped out into the hall to answer. When he returned, the expression on his face was one of concern.

"What's happened?" asked Lars.

"That was Knight. Laura Pritchard has been found dead. She's in the morgue and Scotland Yard has classified it as suspicious. I asked Knight to start running down everything we can find out about her."

"Let him know she was involved with Anton Petrov."

"Shit," swore Björn, softly.

Lars nodded, and for the next several hours, he held Rhys and let her slumber, purring to her whenever she started to wake and lulling her back to sleep whenever she started to rouse. He watched through the window as the Aurora Borealis danced across the night sky. Lars knew there was nothing sacred or paranormal about the display—merely collisions between the sun's electrically charged particles and the Earth's atmosphere. Knowing that scientific explanation had never diminished his fascination with the dazzling display of colors—green, pink, blue, and violet being most common. He liked to believe they were torches held by his ancestors in Valhalla as they danced the night away. He made himself comfortable and held his mate as she slept and mused about all that had brought them both to this place and time.

CHAPTER 22

Rubbing her nose against something warm, inhaling the clean, masculine scent of Lars Jakobsson, ever so gently, Rhys came back to the land of the living—a place Maeve no longer existed. *Maeve.* Her heart twisted.

Lars softly snored next to her. Some badass tigress she turned out to be. She'd fallen asleep in his lap after her crying jag, getting drool and snot all over him, she was sure. But there had been something so safe and secure about being wrapped up in his arms, hearing him croon to her and feeling his soothing purr wrapping its seductive tendrils around her.

She needed to move before he woke, but remaining where she was seemed like such a better idea. She needed to get out of his lap, off his estate and out of the country, but where would she go? She had no identification, no money, no credit cards—

what the hell was she supposed to do? And even if she did, how was she supposed to find Maeve's killer? She wasn't a trained investigator and had no connections with anyone. Those she knew from her own circle of business associates now thought her a thief. Whoever was trying to frame her had seen to that.

Her initial plan to remain with him until she found a way to put her world right again seemed the safest play, but was it? He'd stolen her humanity, but the gift he'd given her far exceeded the cost. The problem was, he believed her to be his fated mate and had no intention of giving her up. He'd made that abundantly clear. When had that prospect begun to have some appeal?

Maeve was dead. Rhys was all alone in the world, but she didn't have to be. She could stay here and be a part of his clan, build a life with him, maybe even come to love him. Or maybe that last part had already begun. She was still pissed at him for the way he'd co-opted her life, but would the alternative be such a bad life?

She breathed him in and her nipples puckered in response. If she didn't get off his lap she was going to start dripping all over him. He was simply the most gorgeous specimen of masculine perfection she'd ever seen. And what he could do with his hands, mouth, and cock ought to be illegal.

The purr became deeper and resonant. It was so tempting to put her head back on his shoulder and accept the solace he offered. Lars laid his hand gently on the side of her head, encouraging her to do just that.

"Rest, Rhys."

"No. I need to know what happened to Maeve. Did you ever let Knight know about Laura's boyfriend?"

"We did. Shortly after we talked about it, Björn spoke with Knight. I've also asked Knight to keep an eye on what's happening as far as the Raphael's whereabouts."

The calming emotions flowing down the tether were intermixed with something else. Rhys tried to identify it, tried to tease out the feelings one from the other.

"What's happened?" she asked, not bothering to raise her head, and encouraging him to talk by nuzzling the hollow of his throat.

"Word came through while you were asleep. Your friend Laura has been found murdered."

"What?" Rhys came up and out of his lap in an instant.

"I had hoped to know more before telling you. Information is sketchy and Knight is trying to find out all he can."

Laura was dead. Maeve was dead. She no longer believed Lars had anything to do with Maeve's death nor did she think he was responsible for Laura. Rhys walked to the window and looked out. The northern lights were dissipating, running away as the first rays of the sun began to make their way over the far eastern horizon.

"What aren't you telling me?" she asked, closing her eyes and focusing her breathing, sure of what he was going to tell her.

"Scotland Yard is looking at you as a person of interest," he said, his arms wrapping around her.

God, he moved like a wraith. You'd think a man of Lars' stature would make noise as he moved, but he didn't. He had the ability to move like a shadow. As she leaned back against him, allowing the quiet purring to embrace her as surely as his muscular arms, Rhys realized that both made her feel safe.

"What else and why me?"

"They believe, or are at least saying they believe, that she discovered your theft, confronted you, and you killed her to keep her silent while you made your escape. Anton, of course, is playing the bereaved lover and has offered a reward…"

"You mean bounty."

Lars nodded. "Precisely."

"Do people believe I'm capable of killing a friend?"

"Anton has characterized you as business colleagues and that you didn't socialize outside of work."

"He got that only partly right. After they started

seeing each other, I made up excuses not to be around them. I never liked him."

"That makes sense. Knight thinks the whole thing has gone bollocks on Anton and that he killed Laura."

Rhys turned in his arms and looked up at him. "Why?"

"Knight believes there are two Raphaels—the masterpiece and the forgery. I know you said the forgery wasn't very good, but you're trained to spot those kinds of things. I know art, but I'm not sure I could spot a fake, and I'm more educated than most…"

"Not to mention far less trusting."

"That, too," Lars said, chuckling.

Rhys shook her head. "Anton had to know I'd spot a fake…"

"Yes, which is why I think he meant to send you the original. You said his provenance was sketchy. I think he meant to switch the two *after* your authentication. Then he would use me to broker the forgery, which when it was revealed to be a fake, would fall back on me and I would be accused of having stolen the original."

"And my being with you…" she said, turning back around. It was easier to talk to him, if she could lean against his strength and not look at how gorgeous he was.

"No. There is no way they could have known you

would be with me. Maeve was the ticket. They used her to bring the Raphael to me through you."

"And would claim we were working together…"

"…for me. Yes. I think they meant to send you the original and have you authenticate that and then they would substitute the forgery for the original. What I think happened was someone sent you the wrong painting."

"They sent me the fake instead of the real one."

"Precisely. When you spotted it and started to write your report, they had to move fast."

"They killed Maeve and Laura. Let me guess—I supposedly stole Laura's laptop."

"Yes, which was awfully convenient. Her entire place was ransacked. It looks like the work of someone who has become mentally unstable."

Rhys pounded the back of her head against Lars' chest. "Why put that out there?"

"So, anything you say in your defense won't be believed. If they can manage it, they'll get you killed either before you're arrested…"

"Maybe I'll 'conveniently' kill myself, leaving a full confession in my suicide note."

She looked up and behind her to see Lars grinning. "That would certainly be the most accommodating thing you could do. But they'll settle for something happening when you are arrested, or they have you cornered. For instance, your head could hit a rock on the ground. Or after you're taken into custody, some mishap could occur. But if they don't manage that and can't get you convicted…"

"They'll get me committed."

"Now, you're thinking like the bratva. Our job…"

"That's 'our' as in me included, right?"

"Short of chaining you to the bed, would I be able to stop you?"

"No, but I won't be a liability, Lars. I know art. I can tell the real one from the fake. I can get us into Lloyd's…"

"Doubtful. By now your security clearance, as well as Laura's, has been revoked."

"Probably. But I'll bet our boss' hasn't. Giles is a lazy sonofabitch and often had one of us log in or out for him or look something up that needed his level of authentication. He won't want them to change his password and identifying information because then he'd have to tell them he broke protocol. And Lloyd's of London is all about following protocol."

"You think there's anything on their computers? Can you remote in?"

"I think it's worth checking. If I log in anywhere other than the company's headquarters, it'll send an alert to the head of cyber security, as well as Giles himself."

Lars looked down at her, his eyes widening and nostrils flaring. His eyebrow arched up again and then his shoulders relaxed. "You're telling me the truth, aren't you?"

"I am. I know it sounds self-serving and if it weren't the truth, I might try to tell you that anyway, but it is the truth."

"Do you think this Giles is involved?"

"Doubtful. He's not overly bright. Office gossip says he got the position because his family is old money, and his older brother is an MP and maybe a viscount or earl or something. Most everybody figures out ways to go around him but make him look good. One of the few things he has a talent for is making people think he knows a lot more than he does."

As it often did, grief over her sister's death reared its ugly head, wrapping its claws around her heart and squeezing. She inhaled sharply, closing her eyes to try and stem the tears that wanted to fall again.

"It's all right, Rhys. I know Maeve's death still causes you pain. Truth to tell, there are many here who share your mixed feelings of anger and sorrow that she can no longer be here with us."

Rhys could feel not only the truth of his words, but the raw emotion behind them.

"Were you in love with her?" she asked.

"No," and Rhys could feel the truth of his answer. "There was something about her to which I felt connected. The minute I met you, I knew what it was. She was your family. You are my fated mate, and as such she was family to me, as well."

"I always thought it was odd that such a bright spirit as Maeve chose to work in the shadows."

"I agree. I wonder if she would have remained with Interpol had she lived."

"Did you like her?"

"I did. Your sister, like you, was difficult to dislike. Even when I knew she was a spy, I had no interest in harming her."

"You'd have protected her if she'd asked you to." It wasn't a question but a statement of fact. Somehow Rhys knew Lars' would have gone out of his way to keep her sister safe, even knowing her initial intent to spy on him.

"She asked me that before I had her escorted from the building. I told her I would protect you both. I also told her to have a care for your safety."

Rhys' breath caught as she bit back a sob. "The last time we spoke, she said we needed to talk. I had the feeling she was going to leave Interpol. I think there was a time she enjoyed all the spy games—pitting herself against others when the stakes were so high, but I think it had lost some of its appeal."

"I believe she had come to understand that there were those in Interpol who were far less honorable men than some of the organized crime syndicates she investigated."

"You think she was going to quit for me."

"Partly. I think she'd grown tired of the game. I think she realized that corruption and illegality existed on both sides, and that some, like the bratva, would lay waste to the world to take what they wanted."

"A nice place in Sweden with a bunch of tiger shifters must have seemed ideal."

Lars chucked. "She didn't know about the shapeshifting."

"I think she would have liked it. Maybe my tigress was supposed to be with her."

"No. I don't believe that. She is too integrated into who you are. The two of you are separate, but when you come together, it is a true blending. It is difficult to distinguish where one begins and the other ends."

"So, now what? Do we head for London?"

Lars pursed his lips. "I figure it's that or measure you for a length of chain and set guards on the doors and on the grounds below our windows."

"We're going to fix this, aren't we?" she asked as she leaned against him and shared in his strength and certainty in the same way she did his warmth.

"We will. We will find those who did this to you, your sister and your friend. They will be made to pay—one way or another."

Rhys could recognize a vow when she heard it. She wasn't sure she could reconcile the man with what he did or how he made her feel, but for now she would take it one step at a time. They would return to London and those who had set her world on fire would have it turned upon themselves and be consumed by it.

CHAPTER 23

Rhys watched the sun rise within the circle of Lars' embrace. She could feel that *something* had settled within them both. She was still unsure whether, when all was said and done, she would remain with Lars. She knew her uncertainty concerned him, but he didn't press her.

"They're going to be waiting for us," he said softly. "For the first time since I became alpha to our clan, I have no desire to interact with anyone. All that I want and need, I hold within my arms."

Rhys started to laugh as she turned in his arms, rose up on her tiptoes and brushed his lips with hers. "I would have elbowed you for spouting romantic drivel, but I could feel your sincerity. I want to be honest with you…"

"You aren't certain as to what the future holds. But I am. We are fated mates and if you can believe in nothing else, believe in that. I will be certain enough for both of us."

He had an uncanny ability to understand where her head was at. She supposed that was the tether. In some ways it was disconcerting and in others it was reassuring. Rhys realized she was softening towards him, and he seemed content not to push. Where some might see his over-the-top pronouncements as a way to impose his will on her, she didn't. She knew through the tether that his feelings were just as he stated. He was certain they belonged together. His belief in that was unwavering and unshakeable.

Lars led her into the bath where they took a leisurely shower. As he ran the natural sea sponge with the wonderful smelling bath gel all over her body, she leaned against him, inhaling the fresh steamy water and just luxuriating in being catered to. When he was finished, she did the same for him. He allowed her to explore his body in a way he hadn't done before. When they were finished, they dried one another off and they entered the large walk-in closet.

Rhys shook her head. "This thing is huge. It's bigger than the bedroom at my loft."

"When I had Runestone modernized, one of the things I did was move some of the walls to combine rooms and open it up. I'm sure some thought it was sacrilege, but I wanted our people to be comfortable and have what they need."

"Does everyone live here?"

"Not everyone, but most. Some who work in Stockholm prefer to stay in the city. But one of the other buildings here at Runestone has been converted to a high-tech office so most of our people have the choice to live here and telecommute or stay in the city. The advantage to being here is being able to shift and run as tigers, although we do have to keep watch."

"Is it more difficult with all of the drone and satellite technology?"

"More difficult, yes, but not impossible and one of the reasons we've left so much of the land that isn't used to keep us self-sufficient as forest." Rhys fingered the clothes that had been purchased for her. "If you don't like something, I can send someone into Visby or even Stockholm. I would prefer you not go until we are able to clear your name."

"With my name now linked with yours, I'm not sure it will ever be clear, but I do understand what you're saying. Britt did a lovely job with the clothes."

"Everyone is anxious to meet you."

"I don't know how to do this, Lars. I've never lived like this."

"We will find our own way. One that works for both of us and the clan. I know that your work is important to you. As I said, if you want to set up your own business, we can do that. I know that Catherine DeMedici does similar work to yours—not the authenticating, but the restoration…" Rhys smiled.

She loved restoring old paintings. "That smile tells me you would not be opposed to something like that."

"You need temperature-controlled workspaces, paints, the minerals to make paints. So much goes into it. It's very expensive to set something up like that."

"Good thing for you, your mate is a very wealthy man."

"I met Catherine DeMedici once, just in passing. She's pretty amazing."

"She is also a shapeshifter."

"She's a tigress?"

"No. A wolf-shifter. Turned, just like you. Her mate, Marco, is a friend. If you like, perhaps we can arrange a visit to their vineyard where Catherine has her studio."

"And did your friend ask for his mate's consent?"

"I believe he did, but then, she-wolves are far less difficult than tigresses."

"That's pretty self-serving, don't you think?" Lars growled and Rhys waved her hand. "I don't want to fight. If I remain with you, and I have yet to decide, I would enjoy visiting the DeMedici vineyard, but first we have to clear my name."

Lars nodded. "And make those who killed Maeve and Laura pay for what they did."

They walked down the main staircase and Rhys wondered what it might be like to live in a place like this with a man, who for all she could tell, was in love with her and saw her as his mate. They entered an enormous dining hall. She wasn't sure what she had expected, but it wasn't this. For some reason, she'd expected expensive carpets on the floor, dim lighting and long tables. Instead, it was a room filled with light spilling through the windows, large round tables where groups and families ate food together, served family style. Food which smelled delicious.

"It's all so beautiful," she said, reaching for his hand, which he took and tucked through his arm.

"You are mistress here. You should feel free to change anything that doesn't suit you."

"Let's not jump the gun. One thing at a time."

Lars shook his head. "None of the rest really matters."

"It does to me."

"You are my mate."

"So you keep telling me."

Lars grumbled under his breath and was greeted by everyone they passed. With any other group of people, she was quite sure it would have felt as though it had taken forever to get to their table. But she was included, and people spoke to her as if she had always been among them. There was a sense of peace and belonging once they were seated with Britt and Björn.

"I take it the mistress is happy?" asked Björn.

"It's hard not to have a glad heart in a place this

beautiful and surrounded by people who wish you well."

"We do," said Britt. "There isn't a one of us who isn't happy to see our alpha mated and settled."

Rhys didn't want to mislead anyone, but before she could say a word, Lars said, "Rhys believes the matter of her position here at Runestone has yet to be decided."

"What's to decide?" asked Björn. "She is your fated mate. What else would she be other than mistress to the clan? How could she think otherwise?"

"Because she is being stubborn and refuses to accept what the rest of us know to be true," answered Lars.

"But you will never let her leave."

"It's not his choice," said Rhys.

"It is," stated Björn. "He is the Winter Tiger. He is alpha. His word is law."

"Björn, it does no good to argue with her. I will simply need to find a way to make her accept that we are fated. I will expect everyone to sing my praises while I ply her with sexual favors so that I can persuade her it was her decision."

Rhys looked at him over her coffee cup. "You and your unilateral decisions. If and when I decide to stay, it will be up to me."

Lars took a deep breath, "Whether or not you settle yourself with your destiny is a decision only you can make, but I assure you the decision about you remaining with me was settled long ago."

"No. You don't just get to roll into my life and take over," she snarled.

"If you believe that, sweetheart, you haven't been paying attention."

Björn laughed. "It is best not to argue with your alpha lest he put you over his knee to convince you to stay."

"I would never do that," said Lars in mock horror. "I would toss her over my shoulder, take her to our bed and settle myself between her thighs until she yielded to my intimate persuasion."

Britt rolled her eyes. "They're all a bunch of fucking Vikings."

Björn looked at Lars. "She says that like it's a bad thing."

Rhys found herself laughing, but regarding Lars seriously. She wasn't sure he wouldn't force the issue, and he had the resources to do it. She felt the soothing purr, rumbling down the tether to her as he took her hand in his, kissing her fingers.

"I will give you time to accept your destiny lies with me, but you are my fated mate and you will remain at my side," Lars said with quiet certainty.

"What about my happiness?" she accused.

"You will be happy. I will see to that."

"Why is it you make it sound like a threat?" Rhys asked.

"Not a threat, mate. A promise."

"You're impossible. Regardless of what happens, please know I would never betray your secrets, and I am grateful for the gift of my tigress."

Lars nodded before turning to Björn. "We need to make arrangements to go to London. Rhys needs to get into the Lloyd's building to see if she can find anything on her friend Laura's computer."

"What are you looking for?" asked Björn. "And can't you do that from here?"

Rhys shook her head. "You may not believe this, but I wish that was an option. I have no desire to be arrested or even taken into custody for questioning regarding the Raphael or the murders of Laura and Maeve. I haven't said anything to Lars, but there were a couple of times before I left London that I felt as though I was being watched."

"Because you were," said Lars. "I had people watching and they spotted others."

"Do you have any idea who?"

"Not specifically, but probably whoever masterminded this whole thing. If Anton Petrov isn't behind it, his father is the most likely suspect."

Björn said, "Most likely. It may end up that we owe the Laochra as much as they owe us."

"Laochra?" asked Rhys.

Lars nodded. "Yes, the coalition of shifter-led syndicates in the UK and Ireland. Knight ran afoul of the bratva, and they asked for the help of the

Northern Lights Coalition, which consists of Gunnar Madsen, the Ice Lion, Anders Jensen, the Snow Leopard, and me," he said casually, taking a bite of toast smeared liberally with lingonberry jam. "Rhys had no idea of Anton's connection with the bratva."

"Do you think Laura knew?" Björn asked her.

"I can't believe she did. Laura was a straight arrow, but our boss Giles' honesty could leave something to be desired."

"Rhys said Giles' has an older brother who's an MP…" said Lars.

"Good way for the bratva to sink their claws into him. They can either blackmail the MP with whatever this Giles has done or get rid of the older brother and put Giles in Parliament."

Lars nodded. "As you can see, our trip to London is essential. Check with Knight. Let him know we're coming. He knows the airport we like to use. See if he can arrange for us to use a helicopter to get into London and then back out. It takes less than five hours to fly there, and I want to spend as little time there as possible." He turned to Rhys. "We will have two hours, more or less, to get in and out."

"If there's anything to find, that should be more than enough time. If nothing else, I'll download everything from Laura's and my files and bring it back here."

"Is it safe for Rhys to go with you? Can't someone just hack in from here?" asked Britt.

"No, not the internal files. Lloyd's has a closed system, and their cyber security is top notch. Giles is a lazy sonofabitch so I should be able to use his password and user ID to get what we need, but only if I'm in the building. Otherwise, we'll alert people that we're trying to get in."

"Once we have what we need, we'll get out and you can assemble your documentation from the plane or back here at Runestone," said Lars. "I'll contact Gavan Drummond. He has contacts within Scotland Yard. We'll get the information to the Yard through Drummond."

"I'm sure Knight will be willing to assist," said Björn. "He said to tell you he knows what it's like to have one's mate in the bratva's crosshairs."

"Good. Björn, I want you to stay here," Lars waved off the protest. "I'll take a small detail with me. I don't want to attract attention. If this is the bratva trying to take a run at us, I want you here. Let those in Stockholm know and make sure they are ready for anything. Keep our people close at hand. Make sure we have patrols out."

"Understood. I don't like it, but I understand."

"Let's finish our breakfast. Have the men prepare the plane. We'll meet them in the hangar." As he took Rhys back to their chambers, he said. "We should be back in less than twelve hours. I would suggest comfortable, dark clothing."

"Why does it not surprise me that you are well versed in breaking and entering."

"The advantages of a misspent youth," Lars said with a chuckle.

Once upstairs, Rhys found black leggings and soft-soled boots. She turned to see what might be available as a top and spied a black, V-neck sweater in Lars' things.

"Can I borrow your sweater?" she asked, picking it up.

"You may borrow anything of mine without asking. What is mine is now yours."

Rhys chose to ignore the seductive purr in his voice. "You are not going to make it easy for me to decide to walk away."

Lars tilted her face to his and kissed the tip of her nose, "I will not allow you to walk away, but I will also do everything in my power to convince you to stay." Rhys hung back. "If you don't want to do this, you don't have to."

"No; that's not it. Is there a place for me to change in the plane?"

"Yes, but…"

"Good. Then can we take my clothes? I'd like to stretch out before we get started. How about if I shift and run back along the tunnels to the plane?"

The corners of his mouth lifted in a smile. "How about if we both do that. I would like a chance to run *with* you, my mate, not after you."

Tearing off her clothing, she opened the door and grinned at him. "That will depend entirely on how fast you are."

The silver swirl of energy, time, and magick surrounded her. It was pretty to watch from the outside as someone else shifted, but to have it surround you was what she imagined it was like to have been present when the galaxy was born. Rhys wasn't at all sure that she wasn't actually in some space between earth and infinity where stars, color, and lightning collided to transform her from human to tigress.

Once the transformation was finished, she watched for a split second while Lars stuffed their things in a bag he could carry before calling forth his own tiger. Rhys bounded out of their room with Lars close behind her. He caught up to her easily and together they made their way down to the tunnel that led to the hangar.

Rhys was still new enough to shifting that she noticed all the differences between the way she perceived the world and her tigress did. For one thing, Rhys never paid much attention to walking or the way the ground felt under her feet. Her tigress did. She knew exactly how to run on each surface—polished floor, hardpack ground, stone walkways—and did so with graceful acumen.

She found it simple to drop into an easy rhythm with Lars as they galloped through the tunnels. She made note of the various passages that led off the main tunnel and wondered where they all might go. She made a mental note to ask Lars about it as they loped along companionably.

When they trotted up into the hangar, Rhys noted again how large the building was and that it housed two jets, a propeller plane, and two helicopters. Lars wasn't kidding when he said he was wealthy. She might be able to take a page from Catherine DeMedici's book and set up her own business. That had been a shocker—Catherine was a shapeshifter.

They trotted up the steps and Lars led her back to what appeared to be a conference room. Closing the door, he shifted swiftly and locked it, giving the pilot the go ahead to take off.

"We'll need to buckle up for takeoff," he said, his eyes sweeping over her, and waiting.

Why was it she had the sudden feeling that Lars wasn't planning on joining the others towards the front of the plane? And why was it she was glad of it?

Rhys shifted and regarded her mate's body and wondered when she'd begun to think of him as her mate? It seemed to her that Lars had been as affected by their run as she had. While her nipples were stiff and her pussy soft and wet, Lars' cock was completely engorged, and she could feel the lust rolling down the tether to her.

"Should I bother getting dressed?" she crooned to him as she sat down in one of the seats.

"Only if you want me to tear your clothes off when we get to cruising altitude and the pilot indicates it's safe to move around."

"Are you planning to move around?" she purred.

"Yes, my beautiful mate. I intend to move you from that seat to the table where I will mount you and fuck you all the way to London."

"They say you're a dangerous man, Lars Jakobsson."

"Are you afraid of me, *Skönhet*?"

"Not in the least. Should I be?"

"No. But I am alpha, and you will yield to me."

"You really won't let me go, will you?"

"No, but I swear I will make you happy. I will spend the rest of my life ensuring you want for nothing—materially, physically, or emotionally. But I will not let you go. You are my fated mate, and neither of us will fare well without the other."

From somewhere deep inside her, laughter bubbled up. "Well, shit. Just when I was beginning to convince myself that you were a gangster and a brigand with no moral code, you go and get romantic. It's going to be very hard to hate you. It might take me a very long time."

He grinned. "I am a patient man, *Skönhet*. Take all the time you need. Then I suggest you take more to ensure you get it right."

The way he looked at her made Rhys feel as though she were an ancient fertility goddess and that her acolyte was set to worship her all the way to London. She knew they had a job to do once they were there, but there was no reason not to enjoy the trip.

CHAPTER 24

Lars wasn't sure what had come over Rhys or how long it would last, but he meant to take advantage of every minute of every opening she gave him. Perhaps Björn was right. Given Rhys' level of arousal, the best way to deal with her when she was unsure might well be to take her to bed and make mad, passionate love to her. His cock throbbed between his legs as if nodding in agreement.

He unbuckled his belt and reached over to do the same for her. Leaning down, he scooped her up in his arms and turned to the large conference table. Perhaps he should have one of the conference rooms on one of the jets converted to a bedroom. He disliked flying, but if making love to Rhys on their plane became the norm, he might learn to like it a great deal.

Lars laid her down on the table, running his finger

down the vertical midline of her body from the hollow of her throat to her parted legs. His keen sense of smell confirmed the glistening visual proof of her arousal. Her beaded nipples were standing stiff and proud, just waiting to be sucked.

Rhys had beautiful breasts—large and firm with dusky areolas and darker nipples. At some point he'd make her hold them together while he fucked them as she sucked his cock each time he pushed forward.

He traced her sex, circling her clit and parting her labia as he stroked it. She was more than ready for him. Her sex was soft, wet, and swollen. He tickled the entrance to her core, and she moaned. Yes, she was very ready. He stroked her again. His fingers strummed her clit until he deftly plucked it. Her body arched up, wanting more contact.

"You are my *Skönhet*. My mate. The one I have waited for. Tell me, my sweet tigress, do you want your mate to whisper sweet nothings in your ear as he ever so gently makes love to you?"

"Maybe later. Right now, I'd like to feel your strength and courage. I need to know that I am safe with you in all ways."

"You are, but that doesn't mean that I will always be gentle with you."

"I don't need gentle… not all the time. Sometimes, I need… I crave just raw, animal passion."

"That I have for you in abundance."

Kneeling down at the end of the conference room

table, Lars grabbed her ankles and drew her back toward the edge, hooking her knees over his shoulders. He would give her what she needed, but first, she would give him what he wanted.

"You are mine, *Skönhet*. Never forget that."

Lars took a long lick from the entrance to her core all the way up to her clit where he swirled his tongue around it and back down again. Once. Twice. Three times. Each time his tongue would barely enter her before licking back up to her clit. When she locked her legs around his neck to try and exert some control, he nipped her swollen little nub with just enough bite that it backed her off from the orgasm that wanted to claim her. Over and over, he took her to the precipice and then backed her off until she was writhing and moaning, her hands clutching at his hair as she tried to pull him deeper.

He speared her pussy with his tongue before dragging it out to start the torture all over again. The way her pussy trembled when he touched her made him feel as though he was the most powerful man on the planet, and she was his mate and would yield to him in all things. Licking down, he stroked her pussy with his tongue as he brought his hand up to her clit.

"Come for me, *Skönhet*."

"They might hear us," she mewled.

"Let them. They will know the Winter Tiger has found his mate and uses her for his pleasure."

This time he growled at her instead of verbalizing.

But the command was the same. As he took her clit within his teeth and sucked, he penetrated her core with two fingers, curling them up and stroking her G-spot, before reversing his position to tug and rub at her clit as he fucked her with his tongue, flattening it to lap up her orgasm as she came, calling his name.

He let her ride the crest of her pleasure before adjusting her position so he could crawl up onto the table, settling himself between her parted thighs as she wrapped her arms around him. This was what he liked about Rhys—she wasn't some delicate little thing that he had to be careful of lest he hurt her. She was soft in all the right spots and yet strong enough to take his weight and the pounding he intended to give her.

His cock poised at the opening to her sex, he began to press in. Each time he mounted her, he was reminded that she was tight—that her pussy fit his cock like a glove to his hand. He pulled back before pushing forward again. She would take whatever he gave her and revel in it. Each time he had spent himself in her, her pussy had spasmed all along his length, milking his cock for every drop of his seed.

He dragged back until only the head of his cock was still surrounded by her before driving deep and making her cry out from the depth and strength of his possession. He retreated and thrust back in, over and over, focusing on her pleasure and her response. He stroked her with strong, hard, measured strokes, pounding into her as she clung to him, raking his back with her nails. She was fierce and bold, and he loved everything about her. The idea that he loved her didn't bother him a bit. She was meant for him, and Lars meant to have her throughout this lifetime and all those to come.

Slipping his hands beneath her, he cupped her buttocks to hold her in place. He picked up the pace and began slamming into her, his cock hammering her pussy with reckless abandon and ruthless intent. Each time he drove into her, she fought to keep him inside, fought to make him give up his cum. Rhys cried out his name as her orgasm swept over them both with a ferocity he'd never felt before. The tigress in her mind yowled in pleasure, its lust and need combining with Rhys in a seductive manner he'd never known before.

Harder and harder he rode her until he could feel the pressure beginning again. As her body tipped over the edge of pleasure and into ecstasy, Lars gave a final, brutal thrust, driving deep and holding himself hard against her body as his cock flooded her pussy with a torrent of cum, filling her to capacity and beyond. Her body convulsed in the rapture of their joining, and he allowed himself to collapse on top of her.

A deep well of satisfaction and well-being surged through his system. Nothing had ever affected him as profoundly as she did. There would never be another for him—not in this lifetime or any of those that followed.

"I love you, *Skönhet*. I will never let you go."

He could feel her tigress growl in the dim recesses of her mind, but instead of arguing with him, she whispered drowsily, "Promise?"

"Yes, my tigress. You are home. You are with your people. The rest we will figure out together."

Lars rolled off the table and pulled on his trousers. Taking her in his arms, he moved them to one of the comfortable seats by a window and settled her into his lap. Rhys cuddled into his body, nuzzling him softly before her breathing became deep and even.

Her respite in his arms was all too brief. He took advantage of her dreamy state, making love to her a second time before they reached British air space. He was definitely having one of the jets reconfigured to have a comfortable bedroom installed.

"Lars, how are we going to get to the Lloyd's building? I know you said your friend Knight would have a helicopter waiting for us, but I also know the helipad at the Lloyd's building has very tight security. I know there are two official helipads, but some privately owned buildings have their own."

"And Joshua Knight owns one of those buildings. He's not too far away from Lloyd's. I spoke with Björn while you slept."

"I seem to be able to sleep very comfortably in your lap."

"Which pleases me more than you know."

"How so?"

"If you weren't comfortable with me, I doubt very much you would curl up in my lap to nap. I have to say I enjoy having you there."

She smiled at him—her body and eyes still retaining their relaxed dreamy state. It was one thing for her to look to him for comfort when she slept… quite another when she chose to remain there when she woke.

"So, Knight's chopper will take us from the landing strip to his building and we walk?"

"No. He'll have two SUVs complete with drivers, and I suspect additional personnel in case we get into trouble. I need your word that if something goes amiss, you will do precisely as I tell you. Your safety is paramount to me. If we're discovered and need to move quickly there won't be time for a lot of instructions. You are to do as you're told. You will be protected at all cost. If something should happen to me…"

"I'll go down fighting with you," she stated in a flat, determined tone.

This fierce tigress was indeed his mate, even if she had yet to accept that. "No, you will go with those who can get you back to the helicopter. At that point, those who are protecting you will decide whether to head for Runestone or take you to Knight."

Rhys said nothing, but Lars could feel her stubborn determination to remain with him and fight settling in. A part of him loved her all the more for it; it spoke of her true feelings, but still he would need to remind his people and Knight's that her safety was the only thing to be considered.

A knock on the door to the conference room. "Lars, the pilot said to tell you we are preparing to land. Knight's helicopter is waiting as are his men."

"Tell him to circle the airport while Rhys and I get dressed."

She batted him with her hand. "Did you have to announce to all of them what we've been doing?"

Lars laughed. "Sweetheart, the interior walls of a plane are not nearly as thick as those of Runestone. Trust me, they are well aware that I have been having my way with you."

She rolled her eyes, closing them as she lifted her face to the ceiling and shook her head. "And what are they going to think of their fearless leader screwing some woman on their flight into a situation that could get very ugly, very quickly?"

"They will think their alpha is the luckiest of men to have an intelligent, courageous mate to see to all of his needs."

Rhys snorted as she stood up. Spotting the bag with their clothing inside, she opened it and upturned the contents out onto the table. They spilled out showing the disorganized manner in which they had been put into the weekender.

"You need to learn to pack," she scolded him, mildly.

"Next time, don't be so quick to shift and leave me scrambling to catch up with you. I enjoyed our run through the tunnels."

She nodded. "So did I. I saw several passageways off the main tunnel, I'd like to explore them."

"You've decided, haven't you?" he asked, standing and retrieving the remainder of his clothes.

"I'd like to say no, but it wouldn't be true," she said, pulling on her clothes. "I'm not sure how, when, or why, but I know my place is with you. Isn't there a line from the Bible about going with your mate and living with him and that his people will be mine as well? I've always liked that saying—never thought it would be applicable to me—but I liked it, nonetheless."

"And I believe you—and Maeve, for that matter—were always supposed to be at Runestone. I intend to have her body brought back home for burial."

Rhys shook her head. "No. Maeve never wanted to be buried. She hated dark, cramped spaces. I'd rather she was cremated, and her ashes scattered to the wind."

"Then it shall be the wind at Runestone. I would have her near us to watch over us all," he stated with certainty.

"You're a curious man. Maeve was sent to try and destroy you and yet when you found out she worked for Interpol you didn't kill her, you invited her to leave them and remain with you. You even told her she could bring me along."

Lars shrugged. "I told you; I knew you both belonged with us. I wasn't sure then how I knew that; I just did."

"When did you decide I was your mate?"

He grinned. "When you walked into Baker Street and had every eye in the room riveted on you without saying a word."

"I'm going to miss Baker Street."

"No, sweetheart, you won't. Once we have your name cleared, we will visit as often as you like."

Lars called up to the pilot to let him know they were ready to land. Joining their men, Lars was pleased to see how respectful they were of Rhys and how they put her at ease in their company. After a textbook landing, the plane rolled to a stop and the stairway was let down.

Joshua Knight was waiting and stepped forward to greet them, extending his hand to Lars. "Good to see you. I wish it was under different circumstances."

"They are what they are, but we will see them put straight. May I introduce my mate, Rhys."

"Rhys Donovan. The woman of the hour so to speak. Drummond says the Yard and Interpol have themselves tied up in knots over this," Knight said, leading them toward the waiting helicopter. "I have people standing by at my building. I would suggest leaving the majority of your men here to safeguard the plane."

"Thank you for your assistance. I'm sure you know, but Rhys' safety is the most important thing."

"Rhys can take care of herself," she said.

Knight grinned. "I'm sure she can. My mate likes to point out to me, as does my sister, that we alpha types can be a bit over-the-top when it comes to protecting our mates."

Lars laughed. "Knowing Marley and Peyton, Knight's sister and mate respectively, I'm sure their language was far more colorful."

Knight grinned. "I fear your mate is right. Come along. As Sherlock Holmes used to say, "the game is afoot."

CHAPTER 25

The helicopter ride from the landing strip to the helipad atop Joshua Knight's building was uneventful as was the ride to the Lloyd's building. The three SUVs parked as inconspicuously as they could, but both Lars and Knight were insistent that one was to remain with a driver at the wheel in the alleyway behind Lloyd's.

The city was quiet tonight… or as quiet as any major metropolitan city could be. She supposed at this point of their adventure, ambient noise was welcome. Lars helped her out of the SUV and he, Knight and the other two tiger-shifters gathered by the SUV's side. Before moving within range of the security camera that was pointed at the keypad, all of them pulled down their ski caps with Rhys tucking her hair under hers.

Knight had asked about the security camera on the way over from his building to Lloyd's.

"Lloyd's is a lot of things," Rhys had said, "arrogant among them. The employee entrance is discreet. A lot of people would walk right past it. And there's a kind of caged 'air lock' just inside. You have to be able to key the second code into that pad within sixty seconds of the first and to do that, you have to know where the damn thing is. So, the camera for the employee entrance is not monitored but recorded. If there's an issue, they look at it. If not, it gets deleted and overwritten every twenty-four hours." Lars shook his head in disbelief. "Like I said, arrogant."

As the group began to move towards the electronic keypad, Rhys pulled on one of the gloves used to gather forensic evidence, smiling at Knight who had supplied them all with gloves to use. Before they were within range of the camera at the employee entrance into Lloyd's, Rhys held up her hand to indicate they should stop.

Turning, she said quietly, "At this point, I think we're better off if it's just Lars and me. I would say it would be best if I went alone…" Lars growled softly. "That's what I thought. But the guards are armed only with tasers, and I've always questioned their ability to shoot straight."

Lars chuckled. "I would question their efficacy on a shifted tiger, but your point about less is more inside is well taken."

Knight bowed his head and he and the other two men backed off.

As she stepped up to the keypad, Rhys took a deep breath, "Do you know this is the only even slightly illegal thing I've ever done?"

"Nothing like diving into deep water," he teased, bolstering her confidence.

"Here we go. Stay right behind me through this door and the next. There's a pretty tight time limit before lockdown is initiated and we're trapped."

Rhys punched in Giles' security code, which unlocked the outer door into the alley. Pulling Lars in behind her, she ensured the door was shut. They were surrounded on three sides by ten-foot-tall chain link panels, forming a six-by-six enclosure. There was a chain link top, a three-foot-thick concrete floor and the building's outer wall to complete the cage. Turning around, she quickly found the secondary keypad on the wall to the left of the door they'd just come through. She entered the code a second time, reversing the order of the numbers. When the chain link door popped open, she pushed Rhys through, closing it behind them and breathing a sigh of relief when it clicked and locked into place.

"So far so good. We'll take the freight elevator to the thirteenth floor. While Giles has a lovely view, those of us working for him were stuck in the basement. Once we've retrieved what we need, I'd like to go down to my workspace…"

"I'm sure they've removed the forgery."

"So am I. But if we're lucky, there may be some test results as well as the sample I sent out to be tested sitting in my physical inbox in my workspace. They were due back today."

"Wouldn't they have taken them to Giles?"

"Maybe. While I'm getting the data, you can look for it. It'll be a large, padded manila envelope."

"You know," he said speculatively as she led them to the freight elevator, "for someone who reportedly said she hasn't done this kind of thing before, you're very good at it."

She grinned at him as once again, she punched in Giles' security code in order for them to gain access to the thirteenth floor and Giles' office. They stepped out onto the marble floor, covered with a large, ornate carpet, running down the center.

"The floors below where the worker bees do their thing are very open, and then there are areas that are carpeted. The executive offices are ornate and betray their heritage of wealth and privilege." She paused for a moment. "Whoa. I never knew how much I resented the inherent class system of how the building is set up."

"It's all right, sweetheart. While we get your new workspace set up, why don't you take a look at where our people work and make sure they have what they need to be efficient, comfortable, and know that they are valued."

The sincerity and caring for his clan flowed down the tether to her as surely as the Thames flowed through London—unwavering and sure.

When they arrived at Giles' office, Rhys keyed in his security code and they moved into the space, closing the door behind them. As Lars began a systematic search of the office, Rhys sat behind Giles' desk and booted up his computer. The first user ID and password she keyed in was flagged as incorrect.

Lars regarded her with concern as he recognized she had been blocked out. "Not to worry. He always uses one of two. His wife's name and their anniversary and his dog's name and his date of birth. The security code to gain entry is his own birthday."

"The head of our cyber security team would thump anyone that used such obvious things."

"Again… arrogance."

Rifling through Giles' inbox, Lars grinned. "Look what I found," he said excitedly, holding up a printed out version of Rhys' report.

"That's fine, but I need to find the digitally time coded electronic version to prove we didn't just create that after the fact." She grabbed an unused flash drive and downloaded all the material she could find that pertained to the Raphael. "Got it. Let's go see if our luck is holding."

They slipped back down the hall, making their way back to the freight elevator and down to the basement where Rhys had toiled away the hours working for the corporate machine. She laughed to herself and could feel Lars questioning her mood through the link they shared.

When the freight elevator doors closed, she turned to him. "I think maybe I'm more cut out to be mate to a gangster than I thought. As silly as it sounds, I'm having a really good time. But at some point, could you just take me some place nice for dinner?"

He laughed and pulled her close. "You name the restaurant—anywhere in the world—and we'll go. I promise."

"I'm going to hold you to that," she said happily as the freight elevator's doors opened and they found themselves facing two burly men with automated weaponry.

Standing behind them was Anton Petrov.

CHAPTER 26

This certainly put a wrinkle into their plans and made what had been an outstanding op and evening into something altogether deadlier.

"I thought when I saw Knight's people in strategic positions outside the building, I might find you here," he said in his heavily Russian accented voice. "You will please step out of the elevator."

"How did you get inside?" asked Rhys.

"I'm afraid Laura was not able to withstand my interrogation regarding the building's security."

Rhys inhaled sharply and turned back to face Lars. "Did you know? Of course, you knew. That's how she died, isn't it? This sonofabitch beat her to death, and you let it happen. God, I despise you."

Rhys prayed that Lars could tell her anger and accusation were just for show. She didn't have any sort of real plan for how they were going to get away, but felt that if Petrov thought they were divided, they had a better chance. She also hoped she could give him time to think. Lars was quick on his feet and his mind worked even more quickly.

All of this flashed through her mind as well as the worry that he might not understand. She could sense the minute changes in his body as he called his tiger forward. As the light and color show of the shift began to spin and envelop him, Petrov's men leaped back. Apparently, they were unaware that their deadly adversary had an even more deadly aspect of his personality.

Rhys jumped to the side as the tiger emerged and leapt at the men with the guns. Her own tigress had been waiting and was quick to take over and emerge. She growled at Petrov as she saw Lars dealing with his gunmen, who had lost their guns and weren't doing well at all. Rhys snarled as she allowed the predator to take over completely.

Her tigress may never have known Laura or Maeve, but that didn't stop her from hating the man responsible. She stalked Petrov who was so terrified, he mishandled his gun, dropping it to the floor as he backed away, holding up his hands. Was he so daft that he thought an unarmed man had a prayer against a shifted tiger? Apparently so.

"Stay away," he pleaded.

Rhys shook her head and growled again. In a perfect world, she could have roared, but she feared she might alert the security staff to what was going on. As all the valuable artwork was locked away each night in a vault, the basement itself had no cameras as it was deemed to be not at risk and of no value to the institution.

The smell of blood assaulted her nostrils, and she knew Petrov's men had not survived their encounter with Lars, nor would Petrov survive his with her.

Petrov stumbled backwards, lost his footing and hit the cement floor, landing hard. Rhys showed her teeth, snarling again as she stepped over him, her long, muscled body hovering over his as his urine began to saturate his elegant silk trousers. Rhys jumped away so as to not have to stand in his filth and grimaced at the smell—he had soiled himself as well.

"Rhys no," commanded Lars as he pulled on clothing he had stripped from the dead men. "We need him."

Trying to recover from his embarrassing display of fear, he rallied, "Yes, you need me."

"Not really," said Lars stepping forward, towering over the Russian mobster's son. "You can make things easier for me and I will let the authorities deal with you. Or you can be difficult, and I will allow my mate to tear you limb from limb." He glanced down at the Rolex on his wrist. "I'd say we have a couple of hours before we have to get back to the plane. Will that give you enough time to play with your food, darling?"

She hissed at him in response, sending nothing but

loving thoughts and feelings down the tether. She had to admit, she was beginning to enjoy the bonding link, which Lars had explained existed only between mates and with fated mates was especially strong.

"Temper, temper, my violet-eye beauty. You know how you hate to get blood on your fur."

Rhys crossed to him and rubbed herself along his legs, purring as she wound herself around him, snarling at Petrov every time he moved.

"So, Anton, would you like to make a little video confession for us? Or shall I allow my mate to have her way with you, which will be nothing like how she has her way with me, which is quite spectacular, sensual, erotic, and entirely satisfying. Have you ever had a strong, fierce female give herself completely to you? Of course not. You aren't man enough to handle a woman such as my mate. Trust me, tigress or human, she is a force to be reckoned with."

Rhys moved forward towards Petrov, showing her teeth, but stopped when Lars put his hand on her head.

"What's it to be Anton? Live or die?" asked Lars in a menacing tone.

"You're... you're a tiger," stammered Petrov.

"Only when we want to be. Confess or die?"

"I'll do it."

"Good man. Let's get you ready," Lars said, pulling him to his feet. "Give me your shirt." Anton complied and Lars handed it to Rhys. "As much as I like having you naked, the idea of this piece of shit seeing all that beauty makes my stomach turn. Go put on the shirt, while I get Anton ready for his close up."

Rhys grabbed the shirt in her mouth and trotted off behind a cubicle wall where she gave her tigress her thanks and allowed her to go curl up by the fire. She pulled on Anton's shirt, which came to her knees and buttoned it up. When she returned, Lars had placed Anton in front of a computer with a monitor and camera. Anton was in a chair, tied down in a way which indicated Lars' knowledge of rope and knots. It made her sex tingle.

"Sweetheart," she purred. "Have you ever done any suspension play?"

"No," he said, indicating the ropes. "I've done my fair share of bondage and have studied shibari, but if suspension appeals to you, I know some excellent instructors and we can put hard points in the ceiling of our bedchambers."

"I think it might be fun. So, what do you have planned for this asshole?"

"We're going to record his confession, send it and the documentation we found to a contact a friend has at the Yard. By the time we reach Runestone, you should be exonerated."

Rhys sidled up next to him, hugging one of his heavily muscled arms with both of hers, cradling it between her breasts so that his hand hung directly in front of her mons.

"Such a naughty kitten," he purred.

"True, but only where you're concerned. Does shifting always make you this aroused?"

Lars chuckled, "Only when your mate is close enough to ensure your hungers—all of them—are met. And are you hungry, my beloved?"

"Ravenous," she said, standing on her tiptoes to nip his earlobe.

"Put your motor on idle until we get back to the plane and then I will see both given sustenance." He turned back to Anton. "As you can see, I have far more pleasurable things to attend to than you. We're going to start recording and you're going to confess to all of it."

"You have no way of knowing," started Anton, whose words were cut off when Lars backhanded him, spinning him around in the chair with the force of the blow.

"We know everything and now have the documentation to prove it. Your confession is merely the ribbon around the gift. You will admit to killing Laura after you coerced her into your forgery scheme, which your father planned to use to discredit me. You will also explain that your father either killed or ordered the death of my mate's sister Mara Donohue, whose real name was Maeve Donovan."

As angry and dangerous as his tone was to Anton, he managed to emit a soothing purr down the tether.

He knew what they needed to get from Anton, but Rhys knew it gave him no pleasure to distress her.

He continued, "You will also explain how you planned to have Rhys authenticate the real Raphael and then sell the forgery. And you will also tell them where to find the original Raphael. If you deviate or falter or don't make them believe, I will allow my mate to rip open your belly and feast on your entrails while you watch her as your life slips away. Ready?"

Lars said the last word in an almost cheerful tone. Rhys had to hide her smile. Knowing he had won the day, her mate was enjoying making his adversary squirm. An hour later, his confession videotaped and documented by an affidavit he signed as to its veracity, Lars gagged him and pushed his chair into a corner.

"Now what to do with these two."

"The building has its own incinerator. I say you dispose of the bodies, and I'll get a mop and bucket and get this blood washed up. It'll never pass a forensic unit looking for blood, but at least it won't be obvious."

"Good plan," he said, nodding. "That was quick thinking back at the elevator."

"I figured if I gave you a bit of time, you'd figure out something and after you shifted and had the guys with the guns neutralized, I figured I could go after Anton. By the way, I have no interest in eating anyone's entrails."

Lars laughed and kissed her with a swift, hard passion that left her breathless. "Good to know."

As he grabbed a heavy canvas tarp to roll the corpses onto to drag to the incinerator, she grabbed his arm and made him face her.

"I didn't say it before, but I love you, too."

"I already knew that, but I thank you for telling me. You are my world, Rhys, and I will give it all right back to you."

Between the two of them, cleanup didn't take much time. They used Giles' user ID and password to send Anton's confession as well as the contents of the flash drive and a copy of Rhys' printed report to Gavan Drummond, who assured them he would see that it got into the right hands at the Yard.

Once they exited the building and everyone was loaded in the SUVs and headed to Knight's building, the enigmatic Lion of London, turned in his seat, "I take it you were successful?"

"More than we could have hoped for. Anton and two of his goons met us in the basement."

"Any clean up I need to do?" Knight asked.

"No, the two I had to kill are burning in the incinerator. After having made a full video confession, which was sent to Drummond along with plenty of documentation, Anton is tied and gagged, sitting in a chair facing the corner."

Knight chuckled. "It might have done him more good had it happened more often earlier in his life."

He looked to Rhys. "I am sorry about your friend and your sister."

Rhys nodded, holding back her tears. "Me too but knowing that those who killed them will pay makes it a bit easier."

The helicopter flew them to the airport without incident and Knight walked with them to their plane.

"Thank you again for your assistance. I fear we may well have made things worse for you with the bratva."

Knight shrugged. "I don't know that you did. They know bringing their bullshit to my city will be costly. I rather imagine Uri didn't know anything about it until it went wrong. It's a bit too heavy handed for him. But keep your mate close. I'll advise the others. Any news on the Cosa Nostra group?"

"Not much, but this may well push them to our side. Making war on women will offend their fiery temperaments. Roman has indicated that regardless of the others, we can count on him."

Knight nodded, and Lars escorted her onto the plane. Once they were seated comfortably and buckled in, the plane taxied down the runway and lifted off smoothly, flying back into the rising sun that lit their way home.

EPILOGUE

Palazzo de Amato
Milan, Italy

Lucrezia, Zia to her friends, Amato threw open the floor-to-ceiling French doors to her Juliet balcony overlooking the canal in the Porta Genova neighborhood. She breathed in the smells of her neighborhood—not all of them pleasant. She laughed, tossing back her long curly mane of hair.

"Things must have gone well at the Doge's Palace in Venice," said her younger sister, Rafaella or Raffi.

Zia turned and leaned back against the railing, her luscious curves outlined by her thin, almost transparent, gossamer silk nightgown. "What makes you say that?"

"Because the *Polizia di Stato* and Interpol's systems are going crazy. I'm surprised there isn't smoke coming out of their headquarters in Rome. I know you got the information I wanted, but why steal it from there?"

Zia shrugged. "Same reason I steal from there whenever I can—because the museum director really does believe he is the Doge of Venice. Bastard. I'll teach him to molest young docents trying to learn about the great masters."

"Didn't you kick his balls up around his teeth when he tried it with you?"

"Yes, and he behaved himself as long as I was there. But I stumbled across a survivors' group. Women and girls have reported him over and over but the *polizia* in the city do nothing. I could kill him, I suppose, but then he would only suffer a little bit…"

"He'd be dead, Zia," said Sofia as she entered the room.

The three Amato sisters were a force to be reckoned with. They could often pass for one another by only substituting a wig for their actual hair. Zia's hair had often been compared to a raven's wing; Raffi's to the red in a Tuscan sunset; and Sofia, or Sofi, to the tawny blond mane of an African lion.

"Yes, which would mean he wasn't suffering any longer. This way we have money, and he loses prestige and importance."

Raffi nodded. "His insurance premiums are through the roof. Most really good collections pass him by. Too great a risk, thanks to you, sister dear. I don't understand why they don't fire him."

"When your father is the reputed head of one of the leading bratva families, people tend not to want to ruffle any feathers."

"Except for that woman up in Sweden—you know the one they tried to frame for her sister's murder and the theft of a Raphael."

"Did they ever find it?" asked Sofi.

"They didn't," said Raffi, nodding towards Zia. "But someone else did."

Sofia nodded. "You really do have a knack for pissing people off. I'm sure last night you stole some other amazing painting that some collector on the black market will pay a fortune for." She leaned forward, grinning, with her hand outstretched. "Meanwhile, what did you bring me?"

Zia laughed. It was good to be home.

Read ***RUTHLESS HONOR***, due out August 11, 2022. ***RUTHLESS HONOR*** is part of the ongoing Syndicate Masters series.

- ***THE BARGAIN NEEDS LINK***
- ***THE PACT NEEDS LINK***
- ***THE AGREEMENT NEEDS LINK***
- ***THE UNDERSTANDING NEEDS LINK***
- ***ALLIANCE NEEDS LINK***
- ***COMPLICATION NEEDS LINK***
- ***JUDGMENT NEEDS LINK***

- ***RUTHLESS HONOR***, coming August 11, 2022
- ***FERAL OATH***, coming September 8, 2022
- ***DEFIANT VOW***, coming October 6, 2022

ACKNOWLEDGMENTS

Thank you to my Patreon supporters.
I couldn't do this without you!

Carol Chase
Latoya McBride
Julia Rappaport
D F
Ellen
Margaret Bloodworth
Tamara Crooks
Rhonda
Suzy Sawkins
Cindy Vernon
Linda Kniffen-Wager
Karen Somerville

ABOUT DELTA JAMES

Other books by Delta James: https://www.deltajames.com/

As a USA Today bestselling romance author, Delta James aims to captivate readers with stories about complex heroines and the dominant alpha males who adore them. For Delta, romance is more than just a love story; it's a journey with challenges and thrills along the way.

After creating a second chapter for herself that was dramatically different than the first, Delta now resides in Virginia where she relaxes on warm summer evenings with her lovable pack of basset hounds as they watch the birds of prey soaring overhead and the fireflies dancing in the fading light. When not crafting fast-paced tales, she enjoys horseback riding, hiking, and white-water rafting.

Her readers mean the world to her, and Delta tries to interact personally to as many messages as she can. If you'd like to chat or discuss books, you can find Delta on Instagram, Facebook, and in her private reader group https://www.facebook.com/groups/348982795738444.

If you're looking for your next bingeable series, you can get a FREE story by joining her newsletter https://www.subscribepage.com/VIPlist22019.

ALSO BY DELTA JAMES

Syndicate Masters: Northern Lights

Alliance

Complication

Judgment

Syndicate Masters

The Bargain

The Pact

The Agreement

The Understanding

Masters of Valor

Prophecy

Illusion

Deception

Inheritance

Masters of the Savoy

Advance

Negotiation

Submission

Contract

Bound

Release

Fated Legacy

Touch of Fate

Touch of Darkness

Touch of Light

Touch of Fire

Touch of Ice

Touch of Destiny

Masters of the Deep

Silent Predator

Fierce Predator

Savage Predator

Wicked Predator

Deadly Predator

Ghost Cat Canyon

Determined

Untamed

Bold

Fearless

Strong

Boxset

Tangled Vines

Corked

Uncorked

Decanted

Breathe

Full Bodied

Late Harvest

Boxset 1

Boxset 2

Mulled Wine

Wild Mustang

Hampton

Mac

Croft

Noah

Thom

Reid

Box Set #1

Box Set #2

Wayward Mates

In Vino Veritas

Brought to Heel

Marked and Mated

Mastering His Mate

Taking His Mate

Claimed and Mated

Claimed and Mastered

Hunted and Claimed

Captured and Claimed

Printed in Great Britain
by Amazon